"Our marriage was a mistake"

Ryan nodded his head in agreement, saying coolly, "I'm inclined to think you're right."

"Then you'll agree to a divorce?" Brittany asked, on a note of discovery.

"I never said I wouldn't. If the terms are right."

Of course, she thought. He had known that if he waited long enough, she'd be prepared to pay for her freedom. "I'm prepared to be very generous," she said.

"With Daddy's money?" Ryan interrupted. "No thanks."

She was offended. "It's my money, my investments," she said tartly.

"It's still only money. Or do you refuse to believe that anyone ever has enough cash?"

"I really don't care." Her voice was hard, calculating. "All I want is a quick, quiet divorce. What is it going to cost me?"

LEIGH MICHAELS likes writing romance fiction spiced with humor and a dash of suspense and adventure. She holds a degree in journalism and teaches creative writing in Iowa. She and her husband, a photographer, have two children but include in their family a dog-pound mutt who thinks he's human and a Siamese "aristo-cat," both of whom have appeared in her books. When asked if her husband and children have also been characterized, the author pleads the Fifth Amendment.

Books by Leigh Michaels

LEIGH MICHAELS

brittany's castle

Harlequin Books

TORONTO • NEW YORK • LONDON
AMSTERDAM • PARIS • SYDNEY • HAMBURG
STOCKHOLM • ATHENS • TOKYO • MILAN

Harlequin Presents first edition November 1987
ISBN 0-373-11028-6

Original hardcover edition published in 1986
by Mills & Boon Limited

CHAPTER ONE

UNLIKE most doctors' examining rooms, this one was neither sterile white nor institutional green. But despite the cheery wallpaper and the bright furniture, there was no concealing the fact of what it was. All examining rooms smell the same, Brittany thought, with that peculiarly sharp combination of disinfectant and air freshener.

'And I know it even though I can't smell,' she muttered morosely to herself, and sneezed.

It was the first time Brittany had ever come to the medical clinic which had recently become a part of First Federal Bank as a new service for the employees, and despite the discomfort of her stuffed-up nose, she was intrigued. The clinic was small, but it was well equipped. There had been no one in the small, comfortably furnished outer room waiting to see the doctor. She wondered if the clinic wasn't being widely used, or if it was simply so efficient that no one had to wait. Brittany made a mental note to ask the bank vice-president who was in charge of medical services.

A young woman in a white coat came in with a smile, a clipboard in her hand. 'I'm sorry to keep you waiting, Mrs Masters,' she said cheerfully, and pulled up a chair. 'Everything indicates that you've simply picked up a nasty head cold. It's nothing serious—there's no lung congestion or other complication. So I recommend that you go home and go to bed, drink chicken soup——' She smiled wryly. 'It really does work! I'll give you a decongestant to help, but sleep is the fastest cure for the common cold.'

'All that's fine, Dr Whittaker,' Brittany said crisply.

'But the Governor is coming to dinner tonight, and I have to be on my feet.'

'I see.' Dr Whittaker looked thoughtful. 'I don't suppose you could cancel?'

Brittany shook her head. 'No. It's a long-standing engagement. And I have a Foundation board meeting tomorrow, and——'

'Goodness, do you ever rest?'

'Not often.' It gives me too much time to think, Brittany almost added, but she reconsidered. 'I simply haven't time to lie in bed and wait out a cold.'

The doctor smiled wryly. 'In that case, we'll just have to see if we can get you through it, won't we?' She reached for a prescription pad.

'I appreciate it, Dr Whittaker.' Then, curiously, watching the woman's slim hand as she wrote the orders, Brittany asked, 'Aren't you bored with practising this kind of medicine? I mean, you're obviously a very good doctor. I saw your qualifications before we hired you——'

'And you, too, are surprised that I settled for cream puff medicine?' Dr Whittaker mused. 'That's what some of my colleagues call it, you know. They think all I do is remove splinters and hand out decongestants.' She smiled and handed the prescription across the desk. 'The pharmacy will fill that for you.'

Brittany glanced at it. 'I really am interested in the clinic,' she said.

The doctor raised an eyebrow. 'And I'll bet that's why you never have time to rest,' she speculated. 'You're interested in everything.'

'At least, everything about how this bank operates,' Brittany said. 'I must admit, when my father had the brainstorm about putting a medical clinic for our employees right here in the building, I wondered if he'd gone a little crazy.'

'As a matter of fact, it was one of the best choices he

ever made,' Dr Whittaker assured her. 'Both for the bank and the employees.'

'Oh?' Brittany's hazel eyes were intense on the doctor's face. It was a simple question, but it would have been impossible to avoid answering it, and Sara Whittaker wasn't the first person to be pinned down by those gently demanding dark eyes.

'Just last week I found a fast-moving cancer, still in the early stages,' the doctor said. She sounded a little reluctant to talk about it.

'What happened?' Brittany prompted gently.

'The man stopped in on his lunch hour to get an immunisation, and as an afterthought, asked about a symptom he'd been having. After I'd examined him, I ordered him to a specialist, and within two days the tumour had been removed. There's an excellent chance that he can be cured.'

Brittany raised an eyebrow. 'And if he'd waited——'

'He probably would have died,' Dr Whittaker said baldly. 'He didn't think it was important enough to bother a "real" doctor about!'

Brittany laughed. It was a musical, infectious chuckle, and even the doctor smiled. 'Anybody who thinks you aren't a real doctor hasn't been watching. But I still don't understand——'

'Oh, I was going to be an obstetrician,' said Dr Whittaker. 'But after a while all newborn babies looked alike to me. I wanted variety. With the employees and their families here at First Federal I have as varied a general practice as it's possible to get. Besides, I don't have to worry about office expenses or whether the patients pay their bills!'

Brittany smiled at that. It had probably been her father's best idea; a token payment for each medical service was withheld from the employee's pay cheque, simply to discourage abuse. But the bank itself paid Sara Whittaker's salary.

'And it gives me plenty of time to spend with my daughter,' added Dr Whittaker, and rose. 'But I'm boring you——'

'Of course you're not!' Brittany's interest was firm now. 'I didn't even know you were married.'

'I'm not.'

'Oh—I'm sorry. I——' Brittany was seldom at a loss for words, but this time she was speechless. It had been a long time since she had put her foot in her mouth quite so firmly.

The doctor started to laugh. 'Perhaps I'd better explain,' she said. 'I'm in the process of adopting Amanda.'

Brittany let the silence drag out for a moment, and then asked wistfully, 'Is it hard to adopt a child?'

Dr Whittaker raised an eyebrow. 'You sound very serious.'

Brittany hesitated. 'I am,' she said finally. 'I've been thinking about starting a family, and it seemed that adoption would be the ideal way for me.'

Dr Whittaker smiled. 'If you're doing it because you're too busy to be pregnant—I'm sorry. That was tactless of me.'

Brittany bit her lip.

The doctor sat down again. 'Adoption isn't an easy road. Cute, cuddly babies are hard to find, and as a single parent, I wasn't even in consideration for one. I waited three years for Amanda to be released for adoption. She's six years old and slightly handicapped—which makes two strikes against her, as far as most prospective parents are concerned.'

'I see,' said Brittany.

'You're married, and that's in your favour. Have you ever been pregnant? It sounds like a prying question, I know, but it's one the agencies will ask.'

'Once.' Brittany's voice was soft with remembered pain. 'I miscarried in my third month.'

'That's not good,' said Dr Whittaker. 'When it comes to adoption agencies, I mean. It proves that you aren't incapable of having children of your own, so you'd be further down the list than most.' She looked Brittany over carefully, then said, 'Why not just have your babies the ordinary way, Mrs Masters? Having a miscarriage that early isn't unusual, you know.'

Brittany bit her lip. 'My husband and I don't live together, Dr Whittaker.'

'I see. That does present problems, doesn't it?' She stood up again. 'I'll bring you some information from my agency—heaven knows I collected drawers full of pamphlets while I waited for Amanda. Perhaps you'll find something helpful.'

Brittany picked up her handbag. 'Thank you, Dr Whittaker, I'd like that,' she said, and added, with gentle authority, 'I can give a child a good home, you know.'

'That's obvious to me, Mrs Masters. But the agencies may not see it the same way, especially if your marriage is breaking up. I'm sorry if that sounds harsh—but I've never believed in sugar-coating reality.'

'Honesty is a quality I appreciate,' said Brittany. 'Of course, I hope you'll keep this confidential.'

'That, Mrs Masters, is the thing I do best.' Dr Whittaker's voice was cheerful, but there was a small frown between her brows as she watched her patient leave the clinic.

Brittany stopped at the pharmacy to get the pills the doctor had prescribed. A percentage of that cost, too, would be withheld from her next pay cheque, with the company picking up the rest. And the result, she saw when she reached the executive floor, was less than an hour of lost time—half of which she had spent talking about adoption. To have gone to a 'real doctor', as Sara Whittaker had called the physicians in private practice, would have taken all afternoon, and the bank would have lost her services for half a day——

'Not that I'm worth much in this condition,' Brittany muttered, and sneezed. She stopped outside the walnut door of her office and, making sure that no one was about, ran a gentle hand across the brass nameplate.

'Brittany Masters, Vice-President,' she murmured to herself. It had such a nice ring, and she had worked so hard to earn that title. Harder, probably, than any of the other hundred vice-presidents in the whole First Federal network. They, after all, had only needed to convince the chairman of the board that they were worthy of promotion. Brittany had had to convince her father as well. The fact that Clint Bridges was both chairman and father had not made it any easier for her, despite what a few of the officers of the bank thought.

At any rate, all that was long behind her, Brittany told herself. The political fighting inside the bank would never vanish completely, but she had proved herself now. In the two years since her coveted promotion had come through, she had convinced most of the sceptical ones that she could do her job, that she hadn't got the title only because she was Clint Bridges' daughter. The ones who remained unconvinced just didn't matter any more, she told herself.

Her secretary looked up with a smile. 'Feeling better?' she asked.

'Of course,' said Brittany, and spoiled it by sneezing. 'That reminds me—I want to find out all I can about that clinic—how it's doing, whether it's being used.'

The secretary was jotting notes to herself on her shorthand pad. 'You had some calls, by the way,' she said. 'The crazy lady in Accounts Payable called again——'

Brittany sighed. 'What's she complaining about this time?' she asked. 'Did we use more than the usual number of deposit slips last month?'

'No. It's paper towels this time. Six extra cases, which

she says is an increase of ten per cent. She can't figure out where they went.'

'Tell her the money was extra dirty, and the tellers had to wash their hands ten per cent more often,' Brittany suggested. 'Why is she calling me about it, anyway? Eric Rhodes is in charge of supply.'

'She said he didn't seem to be interested.'

'I can't imagine why,' muttered Brittany. 'The subject is such a fascinating one. Anything else?'

'Mr Bridges wanted to see you.'

Brittany glanced at the clock and sighed. 'I'll go in to see him right now. Pull the Randolph Corporation's file for me, please, and check its deposit and loan balances.'

'Right away, Mrs Masters.' The secretary looked up, with concern in her eyes, as Brittany sneezed again. 'You must feel awful,' she ventured.

'Oh, it's nothing. This, too, shall pass,' Brittany assured her, and thought as she walked down the hall, I only hope I'm right. She stopped at the water cooler and swallowed one of the decongestant capsules, then went on toward the lush corner office suite that belonged to the chairman of the board.

His secretary was on the phone, but she waved a hand toward the door of the executive office.

In the reception room, the carpet was lush and thick, a heavy pile that Brittany's feet sank into. But inside the office, the floor was covered with a tightly-woven, low carpet just the texture of a putting green. And across the room, the chairman of First Federal Bank was lining up a golf ball with his putter.

Brittany waited patiently until the practice shot had been made and missed. 'I've caught you!' she announced.

Clint Bridges sighed. 'And messed up my shot,' he agreed with long-suffering patience. 'This climate is terribly hard on my golf. I'm thinking of moving the whole bank to Phoenix, or some place where the sun shines all year.'

Brittany laughed and dropped into a chair beside the huge carved desk. 'Why don't you leave the bank where it is, and just move yourself to Phoenix, or Pebble Beach, or Palm Springs?'

Clint Bridges scowled, his heavy white eyebrows drawing together. 'Are you trying to get rid of the old man, Britt?' He sounded a little like a wounded tiger; it did not frighten Brittany.

'Of course not, Dad. But if you'd be happier, there's really no reason for you to stay here.' Her voice was gentle.

There was a long, thoughtful silence. Clint sat with one elbow on the arm of his chair, his hand against his cheek. 'If your mother had lived,' he said finally, 'we'd be in Florida right now.'

'Mother wouldn't have wanted you to bury yourself in this office, you know. It's been more than a year since she died, Dad.'

'Fourteen months, actually.' He sounded absentminded. Brittany didn't doubt that he could, if he chose, tell her precisely how many days had passed since her mother had lost her long fight for life.

He looked up, with a forced smile. 'There's no fun in travelling by myself,' he pointed out. 'It's lonely down there——'

'You might find someone else,' she said softly.

There was surprise in the way his eyebrows arched. 'You wouldn't mind?' he asked.

Brittany shook her head. 'Not if she made you happy. You're still a young man, Dad——'

'Fifty-six my last birthday. Not exactly a kid.'

'Just one thing, Dad,' she said earnestly. 'I want your promise that you'll warn me, if you're going to marry a teenager and look for a house near a school——'

He crumpled the top sheet of a memo pad and threw it at her. 'Mind your manners, Brittany,' he ordered.

She gave him a warm smile. 'What did you want to see

me about?' she asked, suddenly all business.

'I can still cancel that dinner tonight, you know, if you don't feel up to entertaining. Dan Curtis would understand.'

'That would be silly. All the work is already done.'

'Nevertheless, it is my party, and it isn't fair to inflict it on you——'

'Dad,' she interrupted. 'I'm not going to cancel. You might as well stop arguing.'

'All right,' he sighed. 'On condition that you go home right now and take a nap.'

'In the middle of the afternoon? Don't be ridiculous!' It was a wonderful line, with just the right touch of delicate horror at the notion of a career woman needing a nap. If she hadn't followed it up with a sneeze, it would have been perfect.

'Either that or I call Governor Curtis and tell him we'll have dinner another time.'

Brittany knew her father well enough to know that it was not an idle threat. Besides, she had to admit that the very thought of her warm bed was an inviting one. 'All right,' she agreed. 'As soon as I finish the paperwork on the Randolph file——'

'Now,' Clint Bridges said sternly. He punched a button on the intercom. 'Nancy, have Mrs Masters' chauffeur waiting for her. She's going home.'

Brittany sighed. 'Yes, boss,' she said meekly, and marched towards the door.

'I have a wonderful idea,' Clint said suddenly. 'How about both of us taking some time off next week and going down to Palm Springs to play golf?'

'Can't,' said Brittany. 'I'm too busy right now.'

He shrugged and picked up his putter. 'Too bad,' he said. 'You could have chaperoned and introduced me to all the eligible ladies. But if you won't go with me, I guess

I'll just have to stay home this winter and look for a teenager!'

The back seat of the Rolls was so comfortable that Brittany almost fell asleep on the half-hour drive from the frantically busy financial district to the quiet little residential street where she lived. The car rode so smoothly, and the driver was so expert, that it hardly seemed like motion at all.

She closed her eyes. She was dreadfully tired, she thought. Dr Whittaker's words came back to her—'Do you ever rest?' the woman had asked.

Not often, Brittany thought. There's too much to think about, too many things that cause too much pain to remember . . .

She was surprised that she had even told Sara Whittaker about the miscarriage. She didn't talk about it much. But there wasn't a day that she didn't think about it.

She had wanted the baby. From the instant she had first suspected her pregnancy she had lived for that child. She had felt marvellous, too, most of the time. Not for her the horrible nausea and irritability and weariness; pregnancy made Brittany bloom.

Ryan had laughed at the change in her. He had been delighted, too, by the thought of a child. At least, she told herself wearily, she had thought he was as excited as she. But that was when he had started staying late at the legal clinic. She had been so busy following the rules that she hadn't even seen what was happening. But in the end, it had made no difference.

The familiar choking pain rose in her throat as it did whenever she thought of the baby that might have been hers, and she swallowed hard and tried to turn her thoughts aside.

An adopted child—hat would be safe to think about. The idea was not a new one for Brittany, but there had never been anyone to discuss it with. Most people would think it was silly, a woman whose career absorbed so much of her, and who never talked about the baby she had lost, wanting to adopt a child. And yet, in the months since her mother had died, Brittany had begun to long for a baby, someone who would continue the family, to take away the awful loneliness she felt sometimes. As an only child, she was the last of the Bridges family, and when her father died she would be alone in the world.

Once, she thought painfully, she hadn't been alone. Once, long ago, there had been Ryan, and the promise of a future together. Then she had suffered the miscarriage, and the shocking loss of their unborn baby had brought their whole marriage down like the house of cards it had been . . .

If only, she thought bitterly, it hadn't happened that particular day. If it had been the day before, or the day after, then Ryan would have been there, and I would never have known about Diana Winslow. Then I could have gone on in cheerful ignorance——

And have been awakened even more rudely, much later, she told herself sharply. For Ryan's affair with one of his clients had been no one-time thing. Brittany would have stumbled across it sooner or later; it was just Ryan's bad luck that his timing had been off on that day. And bad luck for him that his secretary had not been able to still her conscience, and had told Brittany the truth about where he had been that day.

It was funny that she had chosen to tease her father about needing a house near a school, she thought as the car swept through quiet, tree-lined streets, with houses set far back on rolling lawns. For she had searched out this neighbourhood, and carefully selected this house, because of the location. It was not only within easy commuting distance of the bank, but it was surrounded by advantages for children—the children she had been so certain that she and Ryan would have.

Perhaps it was time, she thought, to put all that behind her—to put Ryan finally in her past. It had been two years, after all, since that awful revelation had struck her like an axe. In that time, it hadn't seemed to matter that she was still technically Ryan's wife. As soon as she had recovered from the miscarriage, she had plunged with all her soul into the new job that Clint had given her, and there had been no room in her life for men. Besides, if one man could treat her as Ryan had, what was to say that the next would be any different? Brittany had felt no desire to find out.

But now——

Am I ready to fall in love again? Brittany asked herself. Is that what this desire for a child is really all about? Is it really a new marriage I want, instead?

All men were not like Ryan. There was Eric Rhodes, for instance, one of the young vice-presidents at First Federal. He treated her so gently, with such concern, that it had startled her at first. He was so different from Ryan . . .

The Rolls swept into the long, curving drive and braked smoothly at the front door of a sprawling stone house. The mansion lay in the weak December sunlight like a kitten, soaking up every last warm ray on the bright slate roof, as if to conserve it for the winter ahead. Brittany's Castle, her father had called it, teasingly, when she had selected it to be her wedding present from him, and the nickname had stuck. Though the house had a perfectly good aristocratic name, chosen after days of thought and research, Brittany's Castle it had remained.

And perhaps that had been part of the problem, she thought with new insight, as the chauffeur helped her out of the car. It had never been Ryan's castle. It had never even, really, been his home . . .

Peters was at the front door before she had reached the step, swinging the carved panel wide. 'Welcome home, madam,' he said.

'You must have been expecting me,' Brittany murmured.

The butler nodded. 'Mr Bridges called.'

The hall table held a dozen red roses in a crystal vase, with a small card discreetly tucked in among the greenery. She opened it. 'I'm looking forward to the party tonight,' Eric Rhodes had written. How sweet of him, she thought. It was the first time that she had invited Eric to the Castle, and the first time he had ever sent her flowers. Brittany wasted a moment in regret that she couldn't smell the roses, then shrugged. There would be other parties, and other roses, after all.

She wandered through the downstairs rooms. In the dining room, the table was already laid with crisp white linen, each service plate perfectly polished, each crystal goblet like a prism in the sunlight. In the drawing room, every cushion was precisely in order, the chairs drawn up for easy, comfortable conversation, the flowers arranged, the cocktail tables already in place. In Brittany's small morning room, behind the drawing room, the rolltop desk was closed, concealing the small computer that linked the Castle to the bank, and her basket of needlepoint supplies stood ready beside her favourite chair. In the library, which had become her father's favourite haunt, the cigar box had been replenished, in case the gentlemen wished to retire there after dinner.

She stood in the library door for a moment, looking thoughtfully across the drawing room and down the long hall, thinking about her first days in this house. Love had been young then, and the world was a new discovery. Then it had been Ryan's library, and the shelves had been full of law books——

There's no point in thinking about that, she told herself firmly. It was all false, all a lie, from the beginning.

She climbed the marble steps to the second floor, feeling suddenly exhausted, and hesitated. The closed door at the top of the stairs taunted her. It would have been the nursery, and there—if things had been different—her toddler would now be taking an afternoon nap. It took determination to walk past that door, but she did it. Down the hall, she paused in mid-step before she went into the master bedroom suite.

'That's silly, too,' she told herself firmly. 'It's been your bedroom for two years, and that's a lot longer than you shared it with Ryan.' But it still took a bit of determination each time she stepped across that threshhold.

Her maid was in the dressing room, humming to herself as she shook out a fluffy négligé. 'I thought perhaps you'd feel better if you changed before your tea, Mrs Masters,' she said cheerfully.

Dad at work again, Brittany thought, and smiled to herself. I'm almost thirty years old, and he's still taking care of his little girl. 'Thank you, Felice.'

Felice tucked her into the king-sized bed, propped her up with pillows, and brought her tea. Brittany sipped it thoughtfully and told herself that it was a luxury to be at home in the middle of the day, a luxury to have time to think. Perhaps, if she put it that way, the things that haunted her might stay away today.

She thought about the red roses down in the hall. Was Eric Rhodes just being especially polite, to send flowers to his hostess, or was he becoming particular in his attentions toward her? Brittany smiled at herself. 'What a Victorian way to put it,' she murmured.

'Madam?' The little maid looked up, startled.

'Oh—nothing, Felice. That's all for now. I doubt I'll sleep, but please come up early so I have plenty of time to dress before the Governor arrives.'

After the maid had gone, Brittany set her cup aside and settled down into the pillows, thinking about Eric. He was a wizard at the complicated formulas that kept a bank humming, and when it came to the computers that were the lifeblood of the industry, he could make them do things that even the manufacturer hadn't thought of. But she wasn't quite sure what she thought of him personally. He was nice enough, but——

Felice found her there, sound asleep with a smile on her lips and a hand curved around a pillow, when she came to help her mistress dress for dinner.

'Lovely dinner, Brittany,' Dan Curtis told her. He leaned back in his chair with a contented smile.

'Thank you, Governor.' Brittany glanced around the table, watchful of her guests' comfort. The nap had helped, but she was feeling the strain, and she was glad there were only six at her table tonight, instead of the twenty-four she sometimes entertained here. Thank heaven for the upcoming holidays, she thought; several of the couples on her original guest list were at other parties tonight. And thank heaven for Dr Whittaker's pills. At least she had stopped sneezing!

To her left, Eric Rhodes was chatting animatedly with Mrs Curtis. Beside the Governor, Brittany's Aunt Lydia was listening to Clint, at the foot of the table, diagnosing the economic affairs of the State. 'Don't you think so, Dan?' Clint asked just then.

'Haven't any idea,' Dan Curtis returned amicably. 'I've been too busy admiring your daughter to pay any attention to what you're saying. You're a lucky man, having Brittany to act as your hostess, Clint.'

Clint smiled. 'The shoe's on the other foot, Dan. I'm fortunate to be Brittany's guest. It's her house, you know—she took me in after her mother died.'

'I didn't know that,' Eric said softly, and Brittany nodded. He had been beside her all evening, watchful of her comfort. It was nice, she found herself thinking, to be taken care of like that.

'We miss Anne so much,' Mrs Curtis said softly. 'It seems to me that marriage is the natural state. It settles a man so to be married.'

Not always, Brittany found herself thinking. It hadn't settled Ryan at all.

Mrs Curtis patted Eric's hand playfully. 'You should go and find yourself a wife, young man, and then your career would really take off.'

'That's quite true, you know,' said the governor. 'I find it in government all the time. Married men are more stable.'

'And what about married women?' Lydia Stratman asked softly. 'Or don't they have a place in your government at all?'

The Governor laughed. 'You wouldn't happen to want a job, would you, Miss Stratman? With that quick tongue, I could find a place for you in my press office any time.'

'No, thank you, Governor,' Lydia said placidly. 'I'm quite content to go on as I am. But you didn't answer my question.'

Dan Curtis threw up his hands in mock horror. 'Just promise me this,' he begged, 'don't go to work for the opposition!'

Clint chuckled. 'Tell us, Dan, when are we going to see some action on all these new ideas you promised during the campaign? Now that you've won your second term——'

'Patience, Clint. All things in good time, and most of them will wait till after the first of the new year. But we're already looking about for the right people, and I'm confident we'll have a new team on board by the end of January.'

Lydia sipped her wine and said gently, 'Which is a polite way to tell you, Clint, that he has no intention of giving you any details. We're all friends here, Governor. It's perfectly safe.'

Eric broke in. 'What about the new state ombudsman, Governor? Any progress on that?'

Dan Curtis seemed relieved by the interruption. 'Not

an ombudsman, exactly, my boy,' he corrected. 'A consumer advocate—that's what we're going to call him. Or her,' he added, with a pointed look down at Lydia.

She merely smiled.

'He will deal with any sort of problem a citizen has— whether it's with the government itself, as an ombudsman does, or the other sorts of problems that arise. Faulty products, fraud, companies going into bankruptcy and leaving the consumer holding the bag.'

'I thought the state did all those things already,' murmured Brittany.

'Most of them. But each part of the government took care of one little area, and by the time the consumer found the people who could help him, he was tired of fighting. This is a new concept. We're going to have one person, one office, which deals with all problems and gets them directed to help right away.' He glanced at Lydia again. 'It will take a special person, Miss Stratman. If you'd rather do that than be in the press office——'

Brittany decided she'd better put an end to this, before two of her guests came to blows in her dining room. Whatever had possessed quiet, ladylike Lydia to bait the Governor anyway? she wondered, and put her napkin down. 'We'll have coffee in the drawing room,' she said softly. 'Lydia, if you'll pour——'

Lydia nodded, frowning a little. It was obvious that she had seen Brittany's exhaustion; it wasn't like Brittany to pass on her duties to someone else. Brittany hoped no one else would be as sensitive to it as Lydia. But then Lydia had known her from babyhood; she and Brittany's mother had been fast friends. It was no surprise if Lydia was extraordinarily sensitive to Brittany's moods.

The Governor and Mrs Curtis left soon afterwards, pleading a busy schedule the next day. Clint directed a pointed look at Eric, who had brought Brittany's coffee to her and not left her side since, and said, 'If you don't mind being left alone, Britt, I'll drive Lydia home.'

Eric said quickly, 'Oh, I'll be happy to stay with her till you get home, Mr Bridges.'

Clint's eyebrows drew together, and Brittany could see a lecture coming. She forestalled it. 'It's all right, Dad.'

There was silence in the drawing room for a few moments after the older couple had left. Eric rose and walked the length of the room, turned hastily, walked back. 'Do you think your father suspects?' he asked abruptly.

'Suspects what?' Brittany refilled her coffee cup. She knew better than to consume so much caffeine, but she needed something to do with her hands.

'That I'm in love with you.'

So—here it was, then. 'I don't know why he should,' she said quickly. 'I hadn't suspected it myself.'

He laughed. 'Oh, come on, Brittany! You must have known I wanted to marry you. Don't give me the old this-is-so-sudden routine!'

And now what do I do? she wondered, and wished she felt better and that her head didn't ache so. 'Well, it is a little sudden, Eric,' she parried. 'For a proposal, at least. And haven't you forgotten something?'

'What?'

'I'm already married,' she said gently.

Eric bit his lip. For a moment, he looked like a scolded puppy. 'I know. It's been so difficult for me, loving you as I do, and knowing that you were tied to that—that monster.'

She wondered idly where the description of Ryan had come from.

'I think about you all the time. I want to be with you every minute. I hoped you felt the same about me, and when you didn't make any move toward getting a divorce——' He sighed. 'But then I realised just now that maybe a divorce would hurt your career.'

'It wouldn't do it any good,' Brittany told him. 'And you thought perhaps I was holding on to Ryan until someone better came along? Poor Ryan!'

'You do like me,' he said. 'I can tell it. I can make you smile when no one else can.'

He was right about that, she thought. He was a charmer, and she did enjoy his company. 'That's not a solid foundation for a marriage, Eric,' she said. 'Believe me, I know.'

'But it's a start. I'll wait, Brittany,' he said eagerly. 'I'll wait till you get your divorce.' He looked boyishly pleased with himself. 'I'll go home now, before your father comes back. The way I feel right now, I couldn't keep from telling him!'

'Eric——' He was gone before she could get the words out. Then she smiled a little to herself. She'd have to straighten Eric out in the morning, tell him that she wasn't ready to be engaged until her divorce was final.

Only then did she realize that she had made her choice. She'd talk to Ryan tomorrow too, and get the paperwork started. It was long past time to be free.

CHAPTER TWO

TRAFFIC was heavier than usual the next morning, and Brittany's chauffeured Rolls was caught in the resulting jam. She sat impatiently waiting out the confusion, thinking fretfully that a smaller car might have been able to wriggle through the maze.

She tapped her fingers on the leather upholstery and checked her wristwatch for the tenth time in as many minutes. She hated being late to work, and she certainly didn't want to miss the Foundation board meeting, especially when that was her best chance to talk to Ryan.

Clint wouldn't be very happy about the idea of a divorce, she knew. He felt almost as strongly on the subject of marriage as Dan Curtis did, and to admit that his daughter had made a mistake would be hard on him.

'As though it's all been a honeymoon the last two years,' she muttered, and the chauffeur looked around questioningly.

Brittany shook her head at him. 'It's nothing, Jackson,' she said. 'I'm just getting old and senile, and now I've started talking to myself.'

He allowed himself a smile. 'Sorry to get you stranded, Miss Brittany. I should have gone the other way around.'

She forced herself to relax. 'I'm sure they'll find a way to open the doors without me for one day,' she said, and stared out the window at the traffic. But she didn't see the cars, lined up motionless in straggly rows, or the traffic lights changing uselessly on the corners. She was thinking about Ryan, and about the disappointment her father would feel. He'd liked Ryan, and even come to trust him, something that Clint Bridges didn't do lightly.

He had been hurt badly when Ryan had moved out of the Castle. But even after that, Clint had named Ryan to the board of trustees of his precious Foundation. No, Clint wouldn't take the idea of a divorce well at all.

But Clint also seemed to approve of Eric Rhodes. Eric had moved up the First Federal ladder very quickly, and several times Brittany had heard her father comment on the young man's appetite for responsibility. Even the jobs that no one else wanted, Eric never shrugged aside, and he did his work well. The department in charge of keeping the bank and its branches supplied with stationery, soap, paper towels, and the tons of myriad supplies, was a good example. It was a mundane job, but Eric had accepted it willingly, computerized the whole affair, and had it running smoothly inside of a month.

At least Clint didn't dislike Eric, that was sure, Brittany told herself. And if she did decide to marry him, Eric would stay with First Federal. That, she knew, was the biggest disappointment Clint had sustained. He had so looked forward to having a son-in-law join the bank. But Ryan had said that the legal clinic he was helping to establish needed him. After it was on its feet, he said, he'd go to work for First Federal. But he never had.

Clint had admired his loyalty to the fledgling firm. So had Brittany, at the time. Now she wondered cynically if Ryan had really been loyal to the clinic, or if he'd merely been waiting for Clint to offer the job he really wanted. Ryan would never have been content with a place in the legal department at First Federal.

I wonder what would have happened, Brittany thought, if Dad had offered him a vice-presidency. The legal clinic would have suddenly become unimportant, then.

It was just as well that it had never come to that, she thought. Ryan, if he had once achieved that position of power, would never have given it up. It was difficult

enough to face Ryan once a month at Foundation
meetings, she reflected. If she had been running into him
in the halls of First Federal every day she would have
been crazy by now!

Traffic was moving again, very slowly. The Rolls
edged ahead, and Brittany sank back into the leather seat
with a sigh. At least, she thought, the confrontation
would soon be over. She was relieved to have the decision
made.

And ultimately, she was certain, even her father would
agree that she was doing the right thing, especially if she
married again soon and gave him a grandchild. That
would bring him round, she thought. Clint Bridges was a
world-class softie when it came to babies.

Her secretary saw her coming, and held up the
portfolio that held all the current Foundation matters. 'I
thought you might be running a little late,' she said. 'Dr
Whittaker brought in an envelope for you this
morning——'

'I'll look at that later,' Brittany announced breathlessly. 'Put it on my desk, please.' She had less than ten
minutes before the board meeting started.

Adoption, she thought as she waited for the elevator to
whisk her up four floors to the Foundation headquarters.
Was that what she really wanted to do? Probably not, she
reflected. What she really wanted was her own baby, a
child who would, perhaps, look like her beloved lost
mother, one who would help her to believe that the loss of
her first child had not been her fault.

Adoption would be a last resort, and it was obvious,
from what Sara Whittaker had said, that the agencies
would look at Brittany as a last-resort parent, too.

The board had already assembled; she was the last to
reach the conference room. There were eleven faces
around the polished mahogany table; distinguished
white-haired businessmen and younger men who were

the leaders of the future, all in tailored suits. The women were all prominent in the city; they wore designer dresses. And then there was one young man with unruly dark brown hair, who wore no tie and a yellow sweater instead of a waistcoat under his corduroy jacket . . .

Brittany paused in the doorway, biting her tongue, and wondered if Ryan did it on purpose. Did he take some secret pleasure in walking into the bastion of conservatism flaunting that ridiculous yellow sweater? As if to show that he couldn't be forced to conform?

To be perfectly fair, though, she had to admit that the sweater wasn't precisely awful. It was a creamy, soft colour that suited him. It was just that it was out of place here.

He looked up then, as if somehow she had drawn his attention, though she knew she had neither moved nor made a noise. For an instant she was breathless, as shy as a child again—as she had been the first time she had felt the weight of that gaze, the dark brown eyes intense, searching——

Don't be ridiculous, she told herself firmly.

Ryan had risen, very slowly, as if uncurling his length from the chair, and drawled, 'I see that Mrs Masters——' he glanced at his watch'—the late Mrs Masters has finally arrived.'

Trust Ryan, she thought, to have a nasty comment, and to deliver it with a twist that was somehow made worse by his beautiful manners. He held the chair next to his, and Brittany sat down stiffly, her back straight, without a word. She would not dignify his presence by acknowledging it.

And that was a short-sighted attitude, she reminded herself. She would need his co-operation if they were to get through this divorce without messy publicity. There was no sense in adding fuel to the fire now.

She turned slightly in her chair and gave him a cold smile. Ryan's eyebrows went so high she wondered if they'd ever return to normal.

Then she addressed the white-haired man at the head of the table. 'I'm sorry to be late, Mr Chairman,' she said. 'I was caught in a traffic jam.'

'It's just now ten o'clock,' he said.

'Then perhaps Mr Masters should have his watch repaired,' Brittany said sweetly.

The chairman tapped the gavel. 'The meeting will come to order,' he said.

For the next few minutes Brittany let her mind wander, as the paperwork that had accumulated since the last meeting was disposed of. Beside her, Ryan was inspecting his watch. He shook it once, and held it to his ear as if to make sure it was functioning. Finally, irritated by his fidgeting, she scribbled a note on a slip of memo paper and pushed it down the table to him. 'Would you cut it out?' it demanded.

'Sorry to disappoint you,' he wrote back, in the spiky handwriting she had grown to know so well, 'but it seems to be working perfectly. Tell me, could it possibly be the bank's clock that's wrong?'

She crumpled the paper, answered, 'Here,' when the secretary called her name on the roll, and fell back into a contemplative silence until the treasurer's report had been given.

'Wait a minute,' she said then. 'Isn't that a dramatic drop in income in the last thirty days?'

'Well, yes,' the treasurer admitted. 'We've approved a great many requests for grant money in the last couple of months, and it's required us to cash in some of the certificates and stocks we were holding. Therefore, the cash flow——'

Brittany reached for her copy of the report and ran an experienced eye down the balance sheet. 'This is inexcusable,' she said. 'We need to cut back on the grants for a while, put additional funds into income-producing investments——'

Beside her, Ryan doodled on a memo pad. 'A grant to a deserving individual is also an investment,' he said.

There were a couple of nods across the table. Brittany was irritated. 'I'm only thinking of the future. We're—investing, if you want to call it that—in some very risky people these days.'

Ryan leaned forward. 'Mr Chairman, I would suggest that Mrs Masters be invited to re-read the Foundation's by-laws. It was set up to fund innovations of any kind, with the understanding that breakthroughs often look hopeless at the start. What bank would have invested in the telephone, for instance, when it was still in the experimental stages——'

Brittany was fuming. 'Mr Chairman, it seems to me that it's not necessary for Mr Masters to be rude on the subject of banks. Besides that, I would like to remind him that I'm fully aware of the purpose of this Foundation; it was my father who set it up. Furthermore——'

'And if one grant in a hundred pays off in an improved way of life, Clint will be very pleased,' Ryan added calmly. 'Which, I might add, will never happen if Mrs Masters is allowed to tuck all the dollar bills away down in the vault.'

She turned to face him. 'If you're trying to work yourself out of a job,' she said politely, 'you're going about it in the proper way.'

Ryan raised an eyebrow. 'Is that a threat?'

'Of course not. I merely meant that if this board keeps spending capital at this rate, there won't be a Foundation by the end of next year.'

'May I remind you, Mrs Masters, that the very money we're quarrelling about was invested in those certificates and stocks last year because we did not choose to award all the grants we were able to give.'

'A foundation should never spend a dime more than its income,' said Brittany adamantly.

'That *is* income. Last year's income.' Ryan shook his head. 'Now I understand why my checking account is always overdrawn.'

'Because you spend more than you make.'

'No. Because bankers are impossible to talk to. They seem to feel that once a penny has crept into their acquisitive little hands, it becomes their private property——'

'Mr Chairman. I take offence at this personal attack,' Brittany complained.

Ryan swept a half-bow in her direction. 'My deepest regrets to the lady banker with the interesting figure—pardon me, I meant to say figures. But you're wrong. Dead wrong.'

The chairman tapped his gavel. 'That's enough, Mr Masters. Mr Treasurer, check back through your records for the source of those funds, and make sure each board member receives a copy of the documentation before the next meeting. Is there any old business?'

Brittany leaned back in her chair. Why, she wondered, did I ever think I loved this man? He's arrogant, rude, hard, unconcerned with other people's feelings——

But he hadn't always been that way.

She propped one elbow on the arm of the deep leather chair and leaned her cheek against it. That first day, she thought, when she had literally run into Ryan Masters on campus, she would never have suspected that this man lay beneath that charming surface.

He had picked her up off the sidewalk where their collision had dumped her, dusted her off, gathered up her handbag and portfolio. She had looked up to thank him, intending it to be cool and crisp—the man had, after all, run headlong into her and introduced her Paris suit to its first sidewalk. But somehow, as her hazel eyes met his dark brown ones, she felt ever so slightly dizzy—as if it had been her head, and not her tailbone, which had made contact with the concrete. She had stammered something. An apology, she rather thought, which was patently ridiculous, since it was he who hadn't been watching where he was going. He didn't answer, but he smiled down into her eyes, and her wobbliness increased.

He had let her hand slip from his, as if reluctant to let her go. She had turned away and then, after half a dozen steps, turned back to find him standing there, silently, still watching her. 'Could you direct me to Williams Hall?' she had asked, almost at random.

He had looked for a moment as if he hadn't heard her. Then he said thoughtfully, 'I could, but it's a bit tricky. It would be easier to take you there. If you wouldn't mind?'

'Of course not,' she said. 'If you have time. I don't want to interrupt your schedule——'

He had smiled again, and suddenly her heartbeat was doing funny things. 'Williams Hall is the economics building,' he observed, as if to himself. 'Are you a new student?'

'No. Actually——' she had told him, with a self-deprecating little laugh, 'I'm a guest lecturer today.'

He had been startled, but he had hidden it well. 'Don't tell me,' he said. Somehow he had managed to get hold of her hand, and now it was resting comfortably in the crook of his arm. 'You're a Nobel laureate who had a facelift—right?'

He had teased her gently all the way to Williams Hall, and when she turned on the steps to thank him for getting her there safely he had refused to take her outstretched hand. 'You haven't told me what you're lecturing about,' he accused.

'It's very dull, really.'

'And you haven't told me who you are,' he added, very quietly.

'Well, that's sort of even, isn't it? I don't know your name either,' she said. When he didn't offer to give it to her, she went on, 'And I've taken enough of your time. You were going somewhere in a tearing hurry when I got in your way. Thank you.' As she turned away, she felt a little lost, as though something precious had just slipped through her fingers.

How silly, she thought. A chance-met stranger, handsome though he was, was hardly anything to break a heart over.

Fortunately, she knew her subject well, and she made it through her lecture without once remembering where she was or what she was talking about. Her thoughts were on that strong face, and the brown eyes surrounded by tiny lines that might have been either worry or laughter. Which? she wondered idly. Was he an instructor? A graduate student? He seemed a little too old for that. What would his subject be? He might be a history buff. Or a writer, perhaps, she thought, remembering his long fingers. A poet, no doubt, she told herself finally, trying to shake the odd sensation that it could possibly matter to her, whatever he did.

She came out of the lecture hall with the last handful of students who had stayed to quiz her, and found him waiting by the door, arms folded, patient. He had taken her hand as if he had the right, and had drawn her away from the students. 'Let me buy you a cup of coffee, Brittany Bridges,' he said. When she had looked up in surprise, he smiled down into her eyes. 'I sneaked into the back of the lecture hall,' he admitted. 'They tell us, over at the law school, that there's always a way to get the information you need. Sometimes you just have to go the long way around.'

Brittany was obscurely pleased. So he had needed to

know her name, had he—not merely wanted it? They drank coffee for hours, and talked, about Brittany and the bank and about Ryan and law school, and how he was older than the average student because he'd had to drop out for a couple of years to save enough money for tuition. He had been matter-of-fact about it; to Brittany, who had never been short of cash, it had been faintly horrifying that he had taken it so calmly.

That night, he had called her at home and they had talked for hours more. And the day after that he had taken her to a free play at the university, and had not apologised because it was all he could afford. It had pleased her somehow.

Oh, he had done a good job of it, she admitted now. He had known precisely how to convince her that he had no interest in Clint Bridges' money. While all the time, that was exactly what he was after . . .

Well, he hadn't got it, she told herself firmly. That was one thing to be grateful for.

'The meeting will stand adjourned,' said the chairman, and rapped the gavel lightly.

Ryan reached for his briefcase and started to put documents and folders neatly into the pockets. Brittany scrambled her papers together into an untidy stack. Her throat was tight. She needed to talk to him, now. But after that sharp exchange during the meeting, would he even listen to her? And if he refused, would he do so quietly, or would he embarrass her in front of the whole board?

'Ryan,' she said softly. 'I need to talk to you.'

For a moment she thought he hadn't heard. His hands didn't pause; the long fingers riffled through the papers in the briefcase. Then, finally, without looking up, he said, 'I thought you'd wiped my name out of your mind entirely. That's the first time you've used it in months.' He looked up then, a hard, speculative look in his eyes.

'What do you want, Brittany?'

'Please don't be hateful,' she whispered.

There was a long silence. He snapped the briefcase shut, and glanced at his watch. 'All right. You want to talk? So talk.'

'Not here,' she said miserably. 'Can I take you to lunch, so we can have a civilised conversation?'

Ryan shook his head. 'No. I have a date.' He picked up the briefcase.

'You'll have to listen some time!'

He turned at the door, one eyebrow raised quizzically. 'I never said I wouldn't,' he said. 'If you want to chat, drop by the legal clinic after work. I'll be there.'

She opened her mouth to refuse, but he was gone. Besides, she thought, what difference did it make? They'd have to do the paperwork some time; he might even set it in motion tonight, and have the whole miserable mess over a little sooner.

She wondered why he wouldn't have lunch with her. A date, he had said. With one of his favourite clients, probably. She wondered if it was still Diana Winslow.

A little flare of anger kindled inside her, and she drowned it out. She hadn't told him that she wanted a divorce, after all. Perhaps, if she had, he would have been eager to talk about it.

Diana Winslow. How could I have been so foolish? Brittany asked herself. No one has such awful legal troubles that they need a weekly appointment with an attorney. Why didn't I realise how much time he was spending with her?

Because it was hidden, she told herself. And because she had been so excited about the baby coming that she had almost forgotten about Ryan. That was why she hadn't noticed when he kept staying later at the clinic, and calling with excuses that got progressively weaker. And she had been so blind that she still wouldn't have noticed, if it hadn't been for Mary Anderson, the secretary, who had come to visit her in the hospital after the miscarriage, and sat there tense and nervous until Brittany had quizzed her.

'I can't stand it any more,' she had said then, as if a dam had burst inside her. 'You're such a sweet child that I can't bear to see what he's doing to you! And I can't lie to you any more.'

Brittany had been astounded that a nonentity like Mary Anderson was feeling sorry for her. The very idea had shocked her, and so she had questioned and prodded till the whole story had come out. Ryan hadn't been in court that day when her pregnancy had ended, as Mary Anderson had told her at the time. Instead, he had been with Diana Winslow. 'He often goes to her house,' the secretary had sobbed, pulling off her heavy glasses to wipe her eyes. 'For breakfast, he said, but he always winked when he said it. And it didn't take a genius to see how it was when she came to the office.'

And that morning, he had told Mary Anderson that he was not to be disturbed for any reason. So, when Brittany had called, she had got the standard story—He's in court, Mrs Masters, I'll see if I can reach him.

And so she had been alone for those first frantic hours, and she had lost the battle to save her baby's life. That wasn't Ryan's fault, of course. Nothing could have stopped the miscarriage, the doctors had told her later. It had been no one's fault. But if he had only been there to hold her——

And that was enough of that, she told herself firmly. She should be glad to know what kind of man she had married, and glad that she was over him and ready to care about someone else.

Eric Rhodes was waiting in her office. 'How did it go?' he asked eagerly.

Obviously, she thought, the grapevine was working

overtime. She was glad that she hadn't mentioned the subject of divorce; if she had, she thought dryly, by now it could have been on the front page of the *Wall Street Journal*.

'It didn't go at all,' she said coolly. 'There was no opportunity to talk about it. Eric, I must remind you that I didn't accept your proposal last night.'

His face fell. 'You didn't? Oh, I see. It wouldn't be quite the thing, would it?'

'It certainly wouldn't. But I wasn't simply being coy when I told you it was sudden. I'm going ahead with the divorce, but I don't want to rush into something new.'

He nodded. 'But unofficially, we're engaged, right?'

She was speechless. 'Eric——'

Clint Bridges tapped on the door and came in. 'Britt, Lydia invited me for dinner tonight. Would you mind?'

'Of course not, Dad.' It makes it easier, she thought. I won't have to explain where I've been, if I go to see Ryan tonight.

Clint looked at Eric with a question in his eyes. 'I didn't know you and Brittany had any joint projects.'

'We're working on some personnel problems,' Eric said calmly. 'I'll talk to you later today, Brittany.'

Clint watched him, with a frown between his eyes. For a breathless moment Brittany thought he was going to give her a lecture, but he shook his head ruefully and said, 'I think I'm starting to see things that aren't there.'

'It's definitely time for a week's vacation.'

'Not if you aren't going along. I'll buy you lunch.'

Brittany shook her head. 'I need to catch up on my work.'

'You also need to eat. Come along.'

Brittany went. There was no arguing with the chairman of the board; what Clint Bridges wanted, he got.

The chauffeur had not been pleased when Brittany insisted on being dropped off in front of the storefront legal clinic where Ryan spent most of his time. 'But how will you get home, Miss Brittany?' he asked fretfully, and shook his head when she mentioned the awful word taxi. 'You call me,' he said firmly, 'and I'll come back and get you. Or if you'd rather, I'll just wait.'

It had been a long time since Brittany had waited for Ryan, but she hadn't forgotten what it was like. 'That would be a waste of time, Jackson. Go on home now.'

The waiting room was crowded; whole families, it seemed, had taken up the vigil there. At a small desk, doing her best to maintain order, was Mary Anderson. She looked even mousier, if that was possible, Brittany thought. It was too bad, she told herself. The woman wasn't all that old, and if she would just fix herself up, get a decent haircut and some glasses that looked a little less like Grandma's, she might be nice-looking. And clothes, Brittany added mentally as Mary Anderson stood up to usher the next client into one of the small back offices where the staff attorneys worked. Definitely the woman would benefit from some clothes that fitted.

The secretary had obviously been surprised to see her. She had seemed to freeze just a little when she looked up and saw Brittany by her desk.

She was a little surprised that Mary Anderson still had a job. But then, she reminded herself, she had never told Ryan that his secretary was the one who had blown the whistle on him. And she was positive that Mary herself would have never had the courage to tell Ryan what she thought of him. And so they all went merrily along, just the same as always. With one difference, of course; Brittany had refused to keep playing the game.

It took two hours to clear the waiting room, and by then Brittany had read every magazine in the place twice. She had been tempted to leave, but had argued herself out of it. She had already swallowed her pride and come here; she might as well follow through.

Eventually, though, the clinic was silent, the last clients being ushered out by Mary Anderson, until only Brittany was left. Even the attorneys had gone, one by one. When Ryan came out of his office, he looked a little startled to see her there.

Did he think he could out-wait me? Brittany asked herself irritably.

'Do you want to come in?' he asked. 'Or shall we kill two birds, and talk over dinner? I assume that you haven't eaten.'

'No, I haven't,' Brittany said sweetly. 'You did say to drop by on my way home from work—and I've been here ever since.'

'Sorry.' He didn't sound it. 'I'll see you tomorrow, Mary.' The secretary's face seemed to tighten at the casual dismissal. Ryan reached for Brittany's arm. 'Come on. My car is behind the building.'

It was dark in the alley, and for an instant, Brittany wondered uneasily if she had made the wrong choice. In the office, Mary Anderson would have been close at hand—just in case.

Just in case what? she asked herself irritably. It wasn't likely that Ryan planned to do away with her!

'Where to?' he asked as he held the door for her. The car wasn't new, she noticed, and it hadn't been a luxury model to begin with. But it was well kept. All of Ryan's things were, she reflected.

'Anywhere. I'm not very hungry.'

'Well, I am. There's a little place a few blocks down that serves good steaks. No atmosphere, of course—is that still so important to you?'

Not under the circumstances, she wanted to say. I wouldn't want my friends to see me! But she bit her tongue. 'That's fine.'

He was right. The little restaurant looked like a converted diner, with garish lighting and tablecloths in a rainbow of colours. But her Bloody Mary was just right—tangy and tart—and Brittany relaxed a bit.

'The legal clinic seems to be doing well,' she observed.

'Evenings are the busiest time. Most people can't afford to take time off from work to consult a lawyer,' Ryan told her. 'Not all of us have banker's hours, you see.'

'I never kept banker's hours.'

'That's true. I'd forgotten that you used to spend all of your time there.'

'You're a fine one to talk! You must like your work.'

Ryan shrugged, and sipped his Scotch. 'You haven't talked to me in months,' he observed. 'I find it hard to believe that you went to all this trouble because you wanted to discuss my job.' His eyes, big and brown, were suddenly intent on her face.

Brittany was intimidated. She stared down at her glass, wondering if this was how it felt to be cross-examined.

'You're right,' she said finally. She shut her eyes tight. Maybe if she couldn't see him when she broke the news, it wouldn't be so bad. 'I—Ryan, I want a divorce.'

The moments ticked by, each second an eternity. She waited till she could bear it no longer, then she cautiously opened her eyes.

'Were you hiding because you were afraid to face the music?' he asked. 'You're something like an ostrich, Brittany.'

She didn't know what she had expected to see in his face. A little shock, perhaps, or some sadness. Or possibly even relief; after so long, he too might want to be free. But there was nothing. Of course, she told herself, Ryan was intelligent enough to know that there could be only one thing that she would want to talk about, and he'd had all day to get used to the idea.

'You're not upset,' she said finally.

'No. Did you think I should be?' The question was sober.

She considered for a moment. 'Not at all,' she said. 'We haven't had any sort of marriage for two years. It's silly to go on pretending, when both of us want to be free.'

'You're no doubt right about that,' he said. 'Or you would be—if both of us wanted to be free.'

She blinked. Surely she hadn't heard him correctly.

The waitress set a plate in front of her. On it, a T-bone steak still sizzled gently. She stared down at the evenly browned french fries and the steaming miniature loaf of homemade bread. The sight would be imprinted in her mind for ever, she thought. Then she looked up at Ryan, her eyes wide.

He answered her unspoken question. 'That's right, Brittany,' he said softly, and picked up his steak knife. 'I did just tell you that I don't want a divorce. I would say that leaves you with a problem.'

CHAPTER THREE

SHE stared at him for a long moment, then she started to laugh. 'Ryan, you always did have the world's strangest sense of humour,' she said at last. 'All right. Now that you've had your joke——'

'I wasn't joking,' he said mildly. 'If I had wanted a divorce, I'd have filed two years ago. Eat your steak; it's best when it's hot.'

Brittany swallowed hard. 'Ryan, don't be ridiculous,' she said faintly. 'You can't want to go on like this——'

'Let's just say that you haven't yet given me a convincing reason to change anything.' He looked up at her, one eyebrow raised, as if challenging her to persuade him.

'I don't see that it's necessary,' she muttered. 'Isn't it enough to say that I'm tired of living like this?'

'Why today?' he countered. 'Why not last month, or next month?'

'Because I don't want to wait till next month. I want to do the paperwork tonight.'

He looked her over casually, as if she were a new suit he was thinking of trying on. 'Have you finally found a man who fits your ideal of a husband better than I did?'

'It wouldn't take much of a search, that's for sure,' she snapped, and bit her tongue.

Ryan eyes were wintry, without a hint of warmth. 'Is he a banker?'

She nodded, then wished that she hadn't.

'I'm sure that pleases your father.' He sliced another chunk from his steak. He looked quite fierce, she thought, like a caveman roasting a chunk of mastodon

41

over an open fire. 'Tell me, Brittany,' he said softly, 'is he more adaptable than I was? I never did quite fall into line as you would have liked, did I?'

'Our marriage was a mistake from the beginning.'

'I'm inclined to think you're right about that, my dear.'

She broke the loaf of homemade bread open. 'Then you mean you will agree to a divorce!' she said, on a note of discovery.

'I never said I wouldn't—if the terms are right.'

Of course, she thought. He had known that if he waited long enough, she'd be prepared to pay for her freedom. She pushed her plate aside. 'What kind of terms do you have in mind?' she asked warily.

'You really should eat your dinner,' he said mildly. 'Alfred is probably watching from the kitchen to see how you like it. And as for terms—what are you offering?'

Brittany obediently cut a bite from her steak. 'That depends on what it's going to take,' she said. 'I'm prepared to be very generous——'

'With Daddy's money,' Ryan interrupted. 'No, thanks.'

Irrationally, she was offended. 'It's my money,' she said tartly. 'I handle my own investments——'

'It's still only money. I'm making quite enough to satisfy my needs—or do you refuse to believe that anyone ever has enough cash?'

'I really don't care, Ryan. All I want is a quick, quiet divorce. What is it going to cost me?' Her voice was hard, she knew. She sounded like a bitter, tough woman, and for an instant she thought she saw a flicker of expression in Ryan's eyes, as if he didn't much like the way she sounded either.

'Haven't you any imagination, Brittany?' he asked. He picked up his glass and swirled the ice cubes.

She drew a painful breath. 'What on earth do you mean by that?' she snapped.

'You want to know what my terms are for a scandal-free divorce so you can marry your new Prince Charming? All right——' his eyes raised from the glass to meet hers, dark and probing, 'I want a job.'

It was something she would never have expected. So, after all this time, he still wanted the position that he had spent so much time and effort trying to get! Well, he was in for a surprise. She said, her voice icy and tightly controlled, 'I will not be blackmailed into having you working at First Federal——'

'I didn't say I wanted to go into banking, Brittany. Corporate law has never been my goal.'

But he hadn't eliminated the idea of a vice-presidency, she noticed. 'Oh? Then what do you want?'

Ryan's eyes dropped to the glass, as if the ice in the bottom of it was some new discovery. 'Your friend Governor Curtis is looking for a consumer advocate,' he told her. 'I want that job, Brittany.'

'Why?' she asked baldly. 'Government service doesn't seem to be quite your sort of thing.'

'Oh, that position is,' he said. 'I like working for the underdog—fighting the big corporations that try to cheat the ordinary person. But most people can't afford to pay a lawyer to fight those cases, so the company wins by default, and goes on to cheat someone else. Governor Curtis has a great idea, and if he can find the right man to run his new department——'

'And you think you're the right man.'

He bowed his head briefly. 'That's right. Your humble servant. You could help me get it, Brittany.'

She started to laugh. 'You might as well go sing to the moon about it,' she told him. 'I don't have that kind of influence with Dan Curtis——'

'Your father does,' he reminded her gently. 'But I don't need influence, yours or anyone else's. I'm well qualified. It's just that the governor has strong feelings about one particular area—and getting a divorce would disqualify me.'

'I don't know what you mean.' But her voice trailed off as she remembered Dan Curtis, sitting beside her last night, saying, Married men are more stable . . . My God, she thought, this is a nightmare!

Ryan had seen the realisation dawn in her eyes. 'I think you do understand,' he said. 'The Governor doesn't come straight out and talk about it, but he only hires married men. You knew that, didn't you?'

'Do you mean that you want to continue this farce of a marriage——'

'I want that job, Brittany. I want it badly enough to do whatever I must in order to have a fair chance at it.'

'So much better a reason to keep the divorce quiet,' she said breathlessly. 'We can do it secretly, with no publicity——'

'I don't think you're listening to me, Brittany. When I said Curtis wants married men, I didn't mean quietly divorced. And he certainly wouldn't consider putting me on his team if I'm in the midst of a messy, brawling domestic squabble——' She flinched, and he smiled grimly. 'Which I promise I will make it if you don't co-operate.'

Brittany sagged in her chair.

'Here it is, Brittany,' he said, and started to tick his points off on his fingertips. 'You want a divorce without a scandal. I want that job. My only chance of getting the job is to present a front of being happily married for a few weeks. And you have no chance of a quiet divorce unless I get the job. Clear enough?'

She was speechless.

'Funny you chose today to ask me about it,' Ryan said thoughtfully. 'I tried to call you last week, but you weren't in.'

'I thought your message was about Foundation

business,' she murmured, scarcely hearing herself. Then she sat up straight. 'Look, Ryan, I have rights. You're an attorney; you know that if you do anything illegal I can have you disbarred——'

He smiled, without humour. 'Certainly I know it. I may not have been in practice very long, Brittany, but I've learned all the ways to tie up the court system, because dragging things out tends to favour the underdog. I could hold up your divorce for at least a year without ever doing anything shady. And then I could ask the judge to forbid you to marry again within the year.'

'That would go for you, too!'

'True. But it wouldn't bother me.' He looked down at his plate, then up again with eyes that were bleak. 'Marriage doesn't seem to be my thing.'

'It wouldn't do your reputation any good, having it splashed all over the city.'

His teeth flashed. 'No—but it would do Prince Charming's even less. Would you care to bet on how many headlines we'd get? Twenty dollars says I can have it on the front page at least once a month.'

She swallowed hard. That was not an idle threat, she knew.

'Don't fool yourself into thinking I'm bluffing,' he said, very softly. 'And if you're considering calling Clint into it, I wouldn't advise it.'

'He doesn't even know I'm here,' said Brittany, unwillingly.

Ryan's eyes brightened. 'Am I to conclude that you haven't told him yet about the divorce?'

'That's right.'

'Smart girl! The easiest way to keep a secret is to share it with no one. It will make it much easier to convince him when I move back into the Castle, and then he can help to convince Governor Curtis——'

'Wait a minute! I haven't agreed to anything!'

Ryan raised an eyebrow. 'What's to agree to?' he asked reasonably. 'All you have to do is put Prince Charming off for a month or two. After I have the job, then we'll go ahead with a very discreet divorce. We both win—right?'

Brittany bit her lip.

The silence lengthened, then Ryan's eyes sharpened. 'Unless there's a reason why you can't wait a month or two?' he asked.

'If you're asking whether I'm pregnant—I'm not,' she said sharply.

'Good.'

'Though I may want to start a family,' she added, with an irrational desire to wound him.

'Why bother?' he asked. 'Why don't you just hire somebody to do that, too?'

Brittany was speechless.

'Actually, I'm glad,' he went on. 'I never was wild about the idea of my kids being raised by a nanny because their mother was too busy to pay any attention to them.'

'It's just as well that you aren't going to marry again,' snapped Brittany. 'You certainly couldn't afford the nanny! I just want to be free of you as soon as possible.'

'Then take my advice,' said Ryan, and signalled the waitress for the bill. 'It will be quick and painless, and both of us win.'

Brittany wasn't so certain of that. 'Isn't this policy of Governor Curtis's illegal?' she asked thoughtfully.

'Absolutely, darling. It's discrimination.'

'Then why don't you just sue him? Make him treat everyone equally.'

In his eyes was the first gleam of humour she had seen all evening. 'That's the problem with you financial wizards,' he drawled. 'You think everything can be reduced to an equation. Knowing that it's illegal is one thing, Brittany. Proving that he's doing it is something else.'

'But just last night he said——' She paused to think about just what it was that Dan Curtis had said.

Ryan said, 'I'd bet my last dollar that he didn't actually come out and say it in front of witnesses.'

He was right, she realised. Dan Curtis had said nothing that would convict him.

Ryan saw the answer in her eyes, and nodded. 'He's too shrewd a politician. All he has to do is claim it's a coincidence that all of his advisers are married. It would be hard to prove that it was intentional. It would take months to make a case, and in the meantime, the job would be gone. I prefer the shorter route.'

'Blackmailing me,' she said tartly.

He looked wounded. 'That's nonsense, Brittany. I've simply notified you that I don't think our marriage is dead.'

'You're leaving me no option, and you know it.'

'Yes, I am. We could go on just the way we have.'

'That wouldn't get you the job,' she said, and could have cheerfully bitten her tongue off.

'That's true,' he said thoughtfully. 'And it also won't let you marry Prince Charming.'

Brittany was darned if she'd admit to him that marrying Eric wasn't in her immediate plans. After all, it was none of Ryan's business.

'So it hardly seems to be an option after all,' she said tightly. Not if she wanted to be rid of him, she thought, and that was becoming more important by the minute. Who knew what his next demand would be?

'I'll pay for dinner,' she said quietly. Ryan didn't seem to hear her, but she saw a muscle in his jaw tense. 'I did offer to take you to lunch,' she explained.

'I'm not quite poverty-stricken, as you so fondly believe,' growled Ryan. He flung a bill down on the table for a tip.

When Brittany saw the size of it, she was appalled, and instantly guilty. I should have kept my mouth shut, she thought. She had never tipped anyone that much in her life; Ryan certainly couldn't afford that kind of gesture!

'If you'd like some time to think about it,' he offered, 'you can call me in the morning with your answer.'

'How extraordinarily generous of you!' Brittany picked up her handbag. 'Now if you wouldn't mind calling a cab for me——'

'I'll take you home,' he said. 'If your driveway wouldn't be insulted by having my car cross it, that is.'

It was a quiet ride. Ryan whistled a little, now and then, under his breath, as if he was pleased with himself and not in the least concerned with what her answer would be. The sound nearly drove Brittany mad.

I don't want to have to listen to him ever again, she thought. I just want to escape him, once and for all, and have this mess behind me!

But what choice did she have? she asked herself. None at all, that she could see. Unless she went along with this charade, what would keep Ryan from making good his threat to create headlines? There was no doubt that he could do it; the Bridges family had always been news, and there were plenty of people who would love to read each ghastly detail of Brittany's failed marriage.

And Ryan, she knew, was capable of giving those details out. It wouldn't hurt him, after all, she thought bitterly; in fact, it would probably bring in new clients!

'I can't stand the headlines,' she whispered, as the car paused before the great front door of the Castle.

She didn't realise she had spoken until his whistle broke off in mid-note. Then he said casually, 'I'll move in just as soon as I can.'

'There's no need to rush!' Brittany snapped.

He lifted an eyebrow. The light above the carved stone arch of the entryway fell in bars across his face, lending a sinister look to each line. 'Oh, but there is,' he said gently. 'I've been away so long, you see. And do have a bottle of champagne on ice, Brittany? We'll want to celebrate our reconciliation in proper style.'

It was all his fault, she told herself the next evening, as she shifted uneasily in her seat in the theatre. If Ryan hadn't tossed that parting shot at her, she might have simply told Eric she couldn't possibly find time to go to a play with him. But Ryan had forced the issue, and so she had found herself defiantly agreeing to this one stolen evening.

Besides, she had told herself, she owed it to Eric to explain what had happened. She could not tell him all of it, she had decided, towards the end of that long and sleepless night. Some day, perhaps, she would confess the whole sordid truth—how she was being blackmailed into resuming this tissue-paper sham of a marriage. But for now she could not put herself so far into any man's power. She had once trusted Ryan, and he had betrayed her. For the moment, she could trust no one.

She told herself that there was no need to tell Eric everything. If they had actually been engaged, she would have had no choice. But as things were, he had far less right than her father to know the truth . . .

And she had lied to Clint. That had been hard. Brittany stirred in the cushioned velour seat and smiled politely as laughter flooded the audience. But she hadn't heard the comic line from the stage. She was thinking about the shock on Clint's face that morning at the breakfast table, when she had asked the butler to refill her coffee cup and added, trying to make it sound like an afterthought, 'By the way, Peters, Mr Masters will be moving back to the Castle.'

The china cup had rattled alarmingly against the saucer, as Peters fought to maintain his rigid control. Then he had said, his face a mask, 'Yes, madam. When shall we expect him?'

'Today, I imagine.'

'Brittany——' Clint had begun, 'I can hardly believe it! I didn't even know you were seeing him——' He got up from his chair and came around the table to give her a fond kiss. 'I'm so glad,' he said simply, hugging her. 'So very glad.'

Brittany's heart had ached at that. It would hurt him even deeper this time, she thought, when the few short weeks were over and Ryan was gone again. But there was no help for it. She was committed now. There was no backing out.

Peters had stopped her later at the front door, as he was holding her coat. 'If I may ask——' the butler said hesitantly, 'which bedroom should be prepared for Mr Masters?'

Brittany had raised an eyebrow. 'He'll be sharing my suite, of course,' she had said coolly, trying to fight down the hammering of her heart. It was the only choice, after all; with Clint living right there in the Castle, it would hardly be convincing if she and Ryan retreated to opposite ends of the house every night. Peters had been more perceptive than she would have expected.

I'll have to watch my step, she thought.

'I forgot to ask Felice to clear out some closet space for him,' she said. 'Would you do that, please?' Peters nodded, and Brittany wanted to add, and tell her to make sure that the couch in the sitting room is ready to sleep on.

Another wave of laughter brought her attention back to the theatre. She tried to concentrate on the stage. Perhaps, she thought, Ryan might not show up after all.

There had been no sign of him yet when she had left the house to meet Eric at the theatre.

The play ended in a roar of laughter, and the curtain dropped to wild applause. Eric reached for her mink jacket. 'You are going to let me take you home, aren't you?' he asked, putting the fur possessively about her shoulders. 'It isn't safe for you to take a cab alone, dressed this way.' He frowned. 'Surely the husband won't grudge me that much.'

Brittany bit her lip. 'I only came so that I could tell you,' she said. 'I'm sorry—I shouldn't have come.'

He caught at the hint of misery in her voice, and misinterpreted it. 'I thought we'd decided everything,' he said. 'And then you turn your back on what we shared——'

'Eric, please. Not here—there are too many people.'

'Very well.' He ushered her out of the theatre and hailed a cab. 'But I don't understand.'

Brittany forced a laugh. 'I don't know myself quite what happened,' she said lightly. 'In fact, Ryan and I were talking about the divorce, and then suddenly we decided to reconcile instead.' She sounded like an idiot schoolgirl, she thought, but what did it matter? Better that than the truth.

'But I love you! And I thought that we——'

She lost patience suddenly. 'I'm sorry if you're disappointed, Eric,' she said. 'But I never led you on. I never even realized——'

'Women!' grumbled the cabbie. 'They're all alike, buddy. Have nothin' to do with 'em, that's my motto.'

Brittany bit her lip and sat silent in the back of the cab, wishing she had insisted on having Jackson wait for her with the Rolls.

At the Castle, Eric said, 'I'm coming in. Wait for me, cabbie.'

'Meter's running,' the cabbie warned.

'Really, Eric——' But Brittany's protest was lost.
Peters opened the great door, and then disappeared
silent-footed down the long hall. She glanced around.
The whole floor looked dark and deserted; it was late,
and Clint would already be in his room. As for Ryan—
well, he might not have arrived at all; he hadn't said it
would be today. She turned back to Eric. 'What is it?' she
asked.

'Just this,' said Eric. His voice had a desperate quality
to it, and he seized her by the shoulders. 'You've brought
this on yourself, Brittany. You've made your choice, and
now you'll have to live with it. But when you find yourself
regretting it—remember this.' His mouth came down on
hers, hard and punishing and yet somehow pleading as
well.

She stayed very still in his arms. Struggling would do
her no good. She wasn't sure she wanted to break free,
anyway. It was rather pleasant to be kissed with such
fierce concentration, as though she was the most
important part of Eric Rhodes' world . . .

Then a calm voice sounded from the dark doorway of
the dining room. 'If you don't want a black eye to show
Clint in the morning, you'd better stop kissing my wife,'
said Ryan, and turned the light on.

Eric jumped, and released her abruptly. Brittany
turned to face Ryan, and saw a look in his eyes that might
have been regret. No spirit, he seemed to be saying as he
looked Eric over from head to toe, and dismissed him.

'I didn't know you'd arrived,' she said feebly.

'I wasn't impressed by the warmth of my reception.'

'Sorry. I don't keep much champagne on hand these
days.' She stepped away from Eric, dropped her mink
jacket across a chair, and started to unbutton one long
glove.

'Your cab is waiting,' Ryan pointed out.

Eric turned obediently towards the door, then caught

himself in mid-motion. 'I'm going to fight for her,' he announced. His voice was low and hoarse. 'I can't believe she prefers you!' He let the heavy door bang behind him.

Ryan stood looking after him for a long moment. 'He won't, you know,' he said conversationally.

'Won't what? Fight for me?' Brittany started on the other glove. 'I wouldn't underestimate him.'

'It would be difficult. You might make a little more effort to be convincing about our reconciliation, by the way.'

'Oh?' Delicately, she stripped the kid gloves from her fingers and laid them on the marble table. He was watching her, she realised, with an intensity that was almost painful. Had she suddenly grown a third arm? she wondered wildly.

'Yes. Such things as kissing your lover in the front hall will have to stop.'

'I suppose you'll give me a black eye as well?'

'Of course not.' Ryan's voice was silky. 'There are far more effective punishments for you.'

She had turned away from him, but her eyes met his in the pier mirror. He looked as if he wouldn't in the least mind dispensing that punishment . . .

Her moment of defiance passed. He could still tell the world what had happened, she remembered—how easily he had hurt and humiliated her. And that she could not stand.

'I won't bring Eric here again,' she whispered.

'And you also won't see him anywhere else.'

'He works at First Federal—I can hardly avoid him.'

'You know what I mean, Brittany.' Ryan's voice was harsh, inflexible.

'My God, you sound as if you're jealous!' she exclaimed.

'Don't flatter yourself. Though if it accomplishes the

purpose——' He sounded thoughtful. 'Shall we go up to bed, my dear?'

Her foot slipped on the bottom step. 'Let's get one thing straight right now,' she said. She was having a hard time getting enough oxygen into her lungs. 'I don't intend for you to share my bed.'

He slipped a hand under her elbow. The brush of his fingers against the delicate bare skin of her arm sent shivers up her spine.

'Don't bother to spell it all out, Brittany. I didn't imagine that you were anxiously waiting for a wild, passionate night in my arms.' His tone was mocking.

She released her breath. At least he was going to be sensible about that, she thought. Once safely inside the sitting room, she gestured towards the couch. 'There's an extra pillow in the closet,' she said. 'And some blankets in that chest. You should be perfectly comfortable.'

Ryan didn't answer. He draped his jacket over the back of a chair and started to unbutton his shirt.

Brittany waited in vain for an answer. Then it occurred to her that if she stood there for another two minutes she was apt to see far more of her husband than she ever wanted to again, so she made a strategic retreat to the dressing room. A chuckle from the sitting room as she pulled the door shut behind her brought a flood of colour to her cheeks.

Ryan was laughing at her, she realized. She seized the négligé that Felice had left for her, and went to take a shower. We'll see, she thought, who gets the last laugh after all!

The rhythm of the everyday routine soothed her into comfort again. She finished with the caress of cleansing cream across her face, lifting the city's grime from her pores, and put everything neatly away. Never in her life had Brittany gone to bed without removing her make-up and tending to her skin. Now, at almost thirty, there was not a line to be found in her flawless complexion. 'Everyday care pays off,' she murmured, remembering what her mother had taught her. Then she yawned enormously and stretched, and stumbled towards the bedroom.

The big bed was shadowed by the drifting lace that draped the canopy. She had furnished the room with abandon, in the days right before their wedding, and only later paused to wonder how Ryan might feel about a bedroom that could have housed a fairy-tale princess. The delicate furniture, the pastels and the flowers, made no concession to a man in the room. She had almost forgotten that he would be living there at all.

He had laughed at the room, she remembered resentfully, and made some remark about it being the perfect place for a Sultan to entertain his harem. It had cut her to the quick, and she had refused to be teased out of her anger. If he hadn't made fun of it, she thought, she might have compromised. But she had stood firm, and ultimately Ryan had capitulated—as he always had— and the room had stayed as it was.

The funny thing was, she realised now, that it had become his room after all. He had been the Sultan, and she the adoring harem of one . . .

Enough of that nonsense, Brittany told herself firmly. It was exhaustion and strain, that was all. That, and the after-effects of her cold, still hanging on. She'd feel better in the morning. She tossed the transparent robe of her négligé across a chair and sat down on the edge of the bed to take off her high-heeled slippers.

'I see you finally threw out some of the doll's house furniture after all,' Ryan said lazily.

She twisted around, eyes dark and horrified like pools in her shock-white face. 'What are you doing here?' she whispered. 'I thought I'd made it perfectly clear——'

'Oh, you did.' He stretched, and sat up, plumping a

pillow to lean against. The sheet had slid to his waist, and his chest was bare. Brittany wondered, horrified, if he was wearing anything at all.

'I took a good look at the couch,' he went on. 'I'm at least six inches longer than it is. I am not going to give up sleeping for a month so you can feel virtuous. Besides, I don't think it would give a good impression of marital bliss if I went around with dark circles under my eyes all the time.' He paused thoughtfully, and added, very softly, 'If I'm exhausted in the mornings, I want it to be because I've been entertaining my wife—not because of a too-short couch.'

'You needn't think I want to be entertained!' She bit her lip. 'I am not sharing a bed with you.'

Ryan yawned. 'Then you might try the couch,' he offered. 'It comes with a good recommendation.' He turned his back on her and slid down under the blankets.

'And I refuse to be driven out of my own bedroom!'

He shrugged. 'Then come on in. There's plenty of room for both of us. As I recall, in the last couple of months that we shared this room, we had no trouble staying away from each other, so we should be quite able to keep our baser impulses under control now.,

'Are you wearing pyjamas?' she asked.

He grinned, then, perfect teeth flashing. 'Why don't you come in and find out?' he invited.

Brittany flung a pillow into the centre of the bed. 'There's the line,' she warned. 'Don't cross it.' She kicked her slippers off and stretched out, pulling the blankets taut over her shoulders.

Ryan seized the pillow and sent it spinning halfway across the room. Then he rolled across the bed until he loomed above her, his hands braced against her pillow, his face dark with anger. 'Let's get one thing perfectly clear,' he gritted. 'I do as I please, and you will not order me around.'

She was terrified. With each beat, her heart seemed to slam against her ribs. He looked capable of murder at the moment, let alone a little matter like rape——

'And the first thing you need to get rid of,' he added briskly, 'is this charming notion that I find your body irresistible. Oh, you're pretty enough—but give me a choice, and I'll take willingness above any amount of reluctant beauty. You're as safe in this bed as you would be in a convent, is that clear enough? Now go to sleep.'

He rolled away from her without waiting for an answer. It was just as well, Brittany thought, for she was incapable of speech. But as she lay tense and listened to his even breathing, she could almost hear her thoughts echoing through the room.

He'll pay for this . . . He'll pay . . .

CHAPTER FOUR

THE winter sun was struggling feebly to break through the December gloom when Brittany woke. She turned over, wondering why she felt so exhausted, and was immediately reminded that this was no nightmare. She had not dreamed Ryan's presence in the big bed.

One would think, she told herself wearily, that after a week of this she would have started to get used to the idea. Certainly by now she could believe the announcement he had made that first night—that he no longer had any interest in making love to her. For in the week they had shared this bed, Ryan had never even touched her.

She fluffed her pillow up, careful to move quietly so that she wouldn't wake him, and stared across the huge bed at him. His face was no less handsome, relaxed as it was in sleep. In fact, without the wary watchfulness that seemed to hover about him in waking hours, he might have been the man she had married. A little older, a little more sure of himself——

Too damned sure of himself, she told herself wryly. And far too conscious of just how much power he had over her.

I should have braved it out, she thought. The newspaper stories, the reporters' questions—they would have been awful, but at least it would have been over with then. It wasn't as if I was in any hurry to be married again. At least by this time I could have been partway to freedom. But now—now anything Ryan wants, he can have. And he knows it. All he has to do is threaten to talk to the reporters.

Perhaps it was fortunate, she thought, that he didn't

58

find her physically attractive any longer. She shivered a little, just thinking about how awful it would be if Ryan had wanted to make love to her . . . if he had coerced or forced her . . .

'Are you cold?' he asked. 'Or scared? Or plotting your revenge?'

She hadn't seen that his eyes were open. The air of watchfulness was back in them, as if he was on constant guard against a hidden weapon. The blankets had slid to his waist, and she was reminded again of the brute strength of his muscles.

His left hand lay on top of the blanket, the gold band on his finger gleaming in the the dim light. After all these years, she mused, he was still wearing that ring. Or, she told herself, more probably he had just put it back on to impress the Governor. But her traitorous memory reminded her of the times she had seen it on his finger—at Foundation board meetings, for instance—without even being aware that she had looked for it. No doubt, she thought, wearing a wedding ring helped to keep the Diana Winslows of the world from becoming too serious a problem.

'What makes you think it had anything to do with you?' she asked tartly.

He smiled, then, and the dark brown eyes seemed to light from within. 'If you hadn't been thinking of me,' he said softly, 'you would have said you were cold. Instead, you attacked.'

'I am cold.' Brittany's voice was sullen.

'Then come here and I'll warm you up.' It was a sensual offer, made in a husky voice.

'No, thanks,' she said. 'I'd hate to put you to all the trouble.' She slid out of bed, rang for Felice, and reached for the terry robe that the maid had left by the bed. She had stopped wearing her delicate négligés, much to Felice's astonishment, and turned to flannel, fleece, and

terry towelling. Glamorous they weren't—and who
cared? Brittany thought. The only one who saw them was
Ryan, and she certainly didn't want to give him any
wrong impressions, as she might have had she kept
coming to bed in lace and chiffon.

Not that he'd been serious about that offer, she
thought. He had no intention of making love to her. If
she had turned to him then, he'd have laughed at her, and
he would have won another battle.

She sat down in front of her dressing table. Felice was
taking an inordinately long time today, she thought, as
she began her make-up ritual. The toner made her skin
tingle as it tightened her pores.

It's not as if I've turned into some sort of hag, she
thought bitterly. I've kept myself in good shape. I look
much younger than my age. There isn't a extra pound
anywhere on me——

Then she realised what she was thinking, and flushed
guiltily. She sounded as if she wanted Ryan to be panting
over her, trying to persuade her to be his wife in more
than name, when in reality there was nothing she wanted
less in the world.

He leaned over her shoulder suddenly and opened the
jewellery case on the corner of the dressing table.

'What on earth are you doing?' she asked.

'I'm just checking to see if you still have a wedding ring
lying around,' he said. 'It would be a nice idea if you'd put
it on. I thought perhaps you'd think of it yourself, but
apparently——'

'I don't want to wear your ring!'

He didn't stop riffling through the compartments.
'You never wanted to wear my ring,' he pointed out. 'It
wasn't elegant enough. That's why you ended up wearing
one your father bought.'

'He only wanted me to have something nice,' said
Brittany. 'It would have looked silly, for me to be wearing

a plain gold band when everyone expected me to have a stunning solitaire——'

'Ah, yes,' he said softly, and put a hand on her shoulder. 'Neither you nor your father ever liked to be embarrassed in public that way, did you?'

It was only a mild threat, but Brittany shuddered. She glared up at him in the mirror.

The little black-uniformed maid appeared in the door. 'I'm sorry to be late, madam——'

Brittany snapped, 'I am not interested in excuses, Felice! Get my cream-coloured suit out, right now.'

Ryan's hand tightened on her shoulder until she almost cried out in pain. 'Do you treat your employees at the bank that way?' he asked.

'What business is it of yours?'

'I just wondered if Felice was the only unfortunate one to get the sharp side of your tongue. I should think you'd be more careful—your image, you know!'

Brittany bit her lip and was silent. I never speak to anyone that way, she thought. But when Ryan is here, I do crazy things.

The little maid had come back into the room with Brittany's suit. 'I'm sorry I snapped at you, Felice,' she said.

Felice bowed her head for an instant, but didn't answer. Instead, she spoke to Ryan. 'Shall I start your shower running, sir?'

Ryan smiled. 'I think I can manage,' he said. 'Be careful, Felice, or you'll spoil me.'

It won a giggle from the maid. That girl, Brittany thought, is on her way out of my employment. 'If you'd like a valet, Ryan,' she said icily, 'I'm certain we can find someone who would put up with all of your interesting little—eccentricities.'

'It would probably be much easier than finding you another maid if Felice decides to quit,' he agreed.

'Brittany, when will you learn that you just can't treat people as though they have no feelings?' He pulled the jewellery case over in front of her. 'I don't care which ring you choose to wear,' he said harshly. 'But so long as I am here in this house you will wear a wedding ring—if only to remind you when you run into Eric Rhodes that you're not free to play around with him.'

'You don't give a royal hoot about Eric!' she snapped. 'All you care about is that Governor Curtis is impressed with how very married we are!'

Ryan smiled. It was not charming, and his eyes stayed hard. 'That's right,' he said. 'After all, that was the agreement. And don't you forget it, because if you do, the cost will be high.'

'It seems to me that you're doing quite a good enough job on your own,' Brittany flashed. 'It didn't take very long last night for you to charm Mrs Curtis into inviting you to stay at Christmas——'

'You weren't listening very well. It wasn't Christmas, it was the weekend before Christmas, and it wasn't me, it was us.'

'Thanks, anyway. I'm not going.'

He raised an eyebrow. 'Really?' he said, and the casual question was more of a threat than violence could have been. 'It should be interesting to see you get out of it, and still convince Dan Curtis that you adore me.'

'Oh, I'll be convincing.'

'Good. And stop trying to change the subject. Get a ring on your finger.' He turned towards the bathroom.

Brittany made a face at the mirror, and then was glad that he couldn't see. There would have been some remark, she was sure. She bent her head over the jewellery case and found her heavy gold wedding band— the one her father had commissioned the jeweller to make, to fit around the fanciful engagement ring she had insisted on. The rings had been connected to form a single unit; she slipped them over her knuckle and remembered abruptly why she had stopped wearing them; it was like carrying a weight around on her hand.

She sat there for a moment and looked down at her hand. The main stone was a star sapphire, an enormous thing that formed the centre of a flower. It was surrounded by diamond petals, and the stem and leaves, also set with diamonds, curved down on to the wedding band. It had cost Clint a fortune.

She and Ryan had fought over that ring. She had designed it, and Clint had indulgently told the jeweller what she wanted. Then Ryan had showed her the severely plain ring that he had bought for her. How silly of him to insist on it, she had said, when Clint wanted to help them out, to get them started. Brittany had laughed at the very idea of wearing that ordinary ring, and Ryan had gone coldly silent——

And then, she thought, he had spoiled the happiest moment of her life by slipping that silly little trinket of his on to her finger at their wedding ceremony, leaving the other ring in his pocket. She had told him he was being ridiculous, as soon as the ceremony was over, and she had refused to go to the reception until she was wearing her real ring.

She stared down at the star sapphire for a long moment. How foolish she had been, she thought now, almost with surprise. How important could a ring be, after all? Surely the valuable part of a wedding ring was not the cost of it, but the care with which it was chosen, and the promise that was made when it was given. Sadness tugged at her as she remembered how radiantly happy she had been that day, as they exchanged the vows that made two people husband and wife for ever ...

For ever, or until Diana Winslow came along, Brittany told herself briskly. Not that it mattered any more. If it hadn't been Diana, it would have been someone else. She

and Ryan were just too far apart, too much different to
have ever been happy together. She had been too young
and too starry-eyed to see it then, but now she knew that
the ring had been the least of their problems.

It was still early when she went downstairs, but in the
hallway, just outside the dining room door, sat a dark-
faced man in a snap-brim hat and an overcoat, waiting
patiently for Ryan. Brittany ignored him. She had seen
him every morning this week; on the first occasion, when
she had raised an enquiring eyebrow at Peters, the butler
had explained, 'He's a private detective, madam. He's
waiting for Mr Masters.'

And there he had been, every morning this week,
waiting to make his report and get his new orders. When
she had asked Ryan about it, he had explained that there
was no point in having a private detective working for
him if every client who visited the office knew what the
man looked like. Brittany had shrugged it off. There was
no point in telling Ryan that she resented having her
house turned into a detective agency. Besides, the man
with the hat certainly wasn't the only stranger that Ryan
had brought to the Castle this week.

Ryan collected unusual people the same way that small
boys brought home stray dogs. He always had, she
realised. In the early days of their marriage, she had
thought it was cute.

Clint was already in the dining room, drinking coffee
and reading the business page. Beside him, demolishing
a plate of bacon and eggs, was another of Ryan's strays, a
thin, freckled boy wearing horn-rimmed glasses. He
looked up with a grin. 'Good morning, Mrs Masters!'

'Jeff, did Ryan invite you to breakfast?' Brittany asked
tartly. Jeff had been hanging around the Castle for days,
but this was the first time Brittany had found him at the
breakfast table. She picked up a warm plate from the
sideboard and helped herself to a toasted English muffin.

'Oh, he told me I should just make myself at home,' the boy said cheerfully.

'I see. Where are you sleeping?' Brittany asked tartly. 'Has he given you a room, or are you just pitching a sleeping bag in the garage?'

Jeff smiled uncertainly. 'Oh, I go home at night,' he told her.

'Surely I can't be blamed for wondering,' muttered Brittany.

'You have the best scrambled eggs around here,' Jeff observed, refilling his plate.

'Really? I haven't tried them in some time.'

'Here. You'll like them.' Jeff dumped a spoonful on to her plate. 'Peters is worried about you 'cause you don't eat.'

'How kind of you both to be concerned.' Brittany stirred the scrambled eggs, and thought about saying something catty. But it wasn't the child's fault, she decided. She tried a bite. Not bad, she decided. Peters filled her coffee cup.

'See?' Jeff asked the butler cheerfully. 'I got her to eat. All you have to do is ask her.'

Peters made a small choking sound, and ignored the remark. Jeff looked confused.

Brittany looked up at Peters, who refused to meet her eyes. Was he really worried about her? There was a warm spot around her heart at the very thought that Peters—stiff-as-a-board, proper old Peters—even noticed when she didn't eat her breakfast!

It was more than Clint did, that was for sure. He refolded the morning paper, laid it aside, and said, 'I'd like to hitch a ride to the bank this morning, Britt, if you're ready to go.'

'Of course.' She gulped her coffee, and gave Jeff a quelling look when he would have protested about the eggs left to congeal on her plate. But she found herself wondering about Jeff, as she half-listened to her father's one-sided discussion on the ride downtown. The child was no more than ten, a thin, gangly youth with a sharp face and a sharper mind. Where had Ryan picked him up? she wondered. And why?

As if he had read her mind, Clint asked, 'Is Ryan planning to adopt that kid?'

'Jeff? I shouldn't think so.'

'I keep tripping over people,' said Clint. 'Not that it's my business to complain; it's your house. Don't you mind that he's filling the Castle with strangers?'

Of course I mind, Brittany thought. I'm furious! But loyalty to Ryan forced her to smile and shrug. 'It's his house, too,' she said softly. Telling Clint the truth would only upset him, and it would make him wonder about the whole situation.

Loyalty, she thought. In the old days, no matter what the problem was, she would have spilled it to her father. She would not have hesitated to tell him what a thoughtless, heartless wretch Ryan was. She could have complained and fussed—

I was a witch in those days, Brittany told herself. It's a wonder Ryan didn't spank me.

'What does he see in all these people?' Clint asked querulously.

Brittany didn't have an answer. She wished she dared tell her father that there was no point in dwelling on Ryan's collection of characters. Ryan would never admit that there was anything strange about them. He would just say that while everyone was normal, some people were a little more normal than others.

'You might tell your pal Eric Rhodes that his Accounts Payable department is causing a whole lot of unnecessary trouble,' Clint said, and Brittany pulled her attention back with a snap.

'Oh? What now?'

'He has a nutty clerk down there who's insisting on chasing down every individual sheet of stationery before she'll approve the bills.'

'She's started bothering you about it now?' Brittany asked apprehensively.

Clint nodded. 'As if I have nothing better to do than worry about how many envelopes the clerical department wastes! If Eric can't calm her down or persuade her to quit making this fuss, I'm going to have to take drastic measures.'

'Perhaps she's a medical case,' Brittany mused. 'Do you suppose, if she talked to Dr Whittaker——'

'It certainly couldn't hurt,' agredd Clint. 'Suggest it to Wonder Boy next time you see him.'

'She's been with us for thirty years,' Brittany said. 'I'd hate to see her fired, after so long, if there's another answer. Perhaps a less stressful job?'

He looked at her oddly. 'What is less stressful than paying the bills for the soap that the janitors put in the employee washrooms?' he asked. 'She isn't doing her job, Britt.'

'I'll talk to Eric this morning.'

'Something has to be done, that's sure,' grumbled Clint. 'She's interfering with my putting practice, and I don't think Eric is taking me seriously.'

Eric looked frantic. He sat bolt upright on the couch in Brittany's office, as though he could not relax. 'I don't know what to do with the woman, Brittany,' he said. 'She's like a cannon gone wild—shooting off blasts in random directions, calling in the top brass. I can't believe that she actually went to see your father. I'd fire her in a minute, but she's been here for ever, and——'

'It just isn't that easy, is it?' Brittany sipped her coffee, and asked, 'You don't suppose she's becoming senile? Or maybe it's a medical problem.'

Eric blinked. 'That had never occurred to me,' he said. 'Britt, you're a genius! It must be something like that. I'll check into it today.'

It was as if he'd received the answer to a prayer. That probably wasn't too far wrong, Brittany thought. Eric had done a wonderful job in that department, but if it started to go bad, he'd get the blame as well as the credit. Banking careers had ended for less reason; Eric was quite right to be concerned about his clerk-gone-wild.

She walked him to the door of her office. He seized her hand, and put a fervent kiss on the back of it. 'You're a darling, Brittany!'

It was a good thing Ryan wasn't around to see that, Brittany told herself. She met her secretary's questioning gaze, and the woman's eyes dropped quickly to the shorthand pad on her desk blotter.

Discretion is the thing, Brittany told herself. She only hoped her secretary had plenty of it!

Suddenly the very atmosphere of the bank was more than she could take. Cold as it was outside, the sun was shining, and the fresh air lured her. 'I think I'll do a little publicity work for the bank today,' Brittany decided. 'I'll be back after lunch.'

She didn't wait for an answer; Susan wouldn't have protested anyway. She wouldn't have dared, Brittany thought, and wondered if Ryan had been right after all. Was she too demanding of her employees?

Then she answered her own question. If I were, they'd stop working for me, she thought.

The little boutique she was headed for was tucked away in a side street. That location, Brittany remembered, had been frowned on by the members of the loan committee. But most of them were men, of course, and didn't understand that half of the charm of an exclusive women's store was for it to be slightly out of the way. Brittany understood it, and so had her friend Alex

Warren, and so Alexandra's Boutique had opened a year ago.

Alex was a redhead who never hesitated to wear the unconventional. The really disgusting thing, Brittany thought when she saw Alex's flowing violet dress, was that, no matter what colour Alex wore, she always looked stunning.

Alex looked up with a smile. 'Brittany!' she exclaimed.

Brittany gave her a hug. 'How's business?'

'Are you here officially, or to shop?'

'I'm doing a little field research today.'

'In that case, I'll tell you that business is wonderful. But before you look at the balance sheets, I have a dress for you to try on. It came in last week and I tucked it away because I knew it was perfect for you.'

Brittany smiled. That consummate salesmanship of Alex's was why she had backed the idea of the business loan so strongly. 'Do you know,' she said thoughtfully, 'I wish sometimes that First Federal hadn't given you all that money.'

'Why?' Alex looked innocent. 'Because I keep expanding your wardrobe?'

'No—because if the bank hadn't made the loan, I'd have bought in as a partner, and I'd be the one raking in the profits. Let's see this marvellous dress.'

'I hid it in the back room,' Alex confessed. 'I didn't want anyone else to even get a look at it.'

The dress was the colour of rich cream, with gold fibres shot through it at random. The fabric was as light and soft as a spiderweb, and the styling was deceptively simple, with a slightly gathered skirt, a demurely draped neckline, and no back at all.

Brittany studied herself in the mirror, then turned to her friend with a raised eyebrow. 'And just where will I wear something like this?' she asked gently.

'To the charity style show next month,' suggested

Alex. 'I even have the gold gloves to match it. Do you
realize how few women really look good in gloves?
You're a lucky girl, Brittany Masters.'

Brittany yielded. It was a beautiful dress, and Alex's
taste, as always, was faultless. 'Send the gloves, too,' she
said.

'And shoes? You'll need some high-heeled, strappy
gold sandals.'

'You're determined to make me regret stopping, aren't
you, Alexandra? All right, the sandals. Now the least you
can do is take me to lunch, away from all this temptation,
so we can talk business.'

'Absolutely,' smiled Alex. She handed the dress over to
an assistant to be boxed and delivered. 'But you'll have to
pay—my expense account is shot for the month.'

As they turned towards the front of the shop, another
customer came from the fitting room. She was tall,
blonde, tanned, and gorgeous, and the mere sight of
her—as it always did—brought cold bitterness to
Brittany's heart, and the memory of a secretary's
colourless little voice as she had said, 'The truth is that he
wasn't in court, Mrs Masters. He was with Diana
Winslow——'

Mary Anderson's words had cut her like knives.
Brittany had refused, at first, to believe the accusations.
But as she had thought it all over, things began to make
sense.

Ryan and Diana. They saw a great deal of each other,
of course, because they went to the same parties, the
same restaurants, the same charity affairs. When Diana
found herself with legal trouble, she had consulted Ryan.
But Brittany had never suspected that it might have gone
further than that. They danced together, of course, as
Ryan danced with all of Brittany's friends. But no more
than that . . .

And then Alex Warren had filled in the pieces. Yes,

she had admitted, under Brittany's questioning, she had seen Ryan and Diana together on innumerable occasions. Lunching together, driving together—at times when it could not have been coincidence.

It was the confirmation Brittany had needed. She had gone home from the hospital, pale and weak. Ryan had hovered by her side every moment, and each time he touched her or even said her name, she wanted to scream at him to leave her alone.

Ultimately, she had done exactly that. She hadn't mentioned Diana's name, though, on that last frightful afternoon; her pride would not allow it. She had told him merely that their marriage had no chance of succeeding, because they were so much different. She told him that she didn't want to see him again, and that when their baby had died, so had their marriage.

He hadn't argued. He had seemed to know, she thought, that she would never change her mind. There was no point in discussing it further; talking about it wouldn't make it go away.

He had moved out that day. Her first thought was that it was over, and now she could get back to normal. She had been so innocent, then, thinking it could all be put behind her. Instead, every time she had seen Diana Winslow in the last two years, she had been tormented all over again.

'Good morning, Diana,' said Alex. 'Did you find what you wanted?'

Did she know? Brittany wondered. Had Ryan told Diana that they were living together again—and why? I can't bear it, she thought, for Diana to know that it's all a farce. It's bad enough that she broke up my marriage, but to have her laughing at me now—it's more than I can stand.

Diana shrugged her pretty shoulders. 'It will do,' she said. 'And you, Brittany? Are you in the market for a new set of négligés, now that your wandering husband has come home for a while?'

Brittany's fingers clenched on her leather handbag. There was a harsh note in the woman's voice; had Diana learned the hard way that Ryan didn't know what it meant to be faithful?

'Don't get your hopes up,' Diana added sweetly. 'He's only taking a vacation, and if you're not a complete fool you know it won't last this time either.'

So perhaps Ryan hadn't told her. Perhaps that affair was finally over, Brittany thought. Then she remembered Ryan saying that the best way to keep a secret was to not share it with anyone. Even her father, he had said. Even Eric—even Diana. It didn't mean a thing.

Diana's eyes sharpened. 'Whatever made you think you were enough of a woman to satisfy him?' she asked. 'A cold little milk-and-water miss like you—Ryan needs life, and spirit.'

Alex stepped between them. 'That's enough, Diana,' she said softly. 'This is a dress shop, not a boxing ring. If you must cut up at Brittany, please do it somewhere else.'

'If you don't want my business, Alexandra——'

Brittany cut in quietly, 'I'm so sorry you feel that way, Diana. It must have been very difficult for you, knowing that Ryan didn't care for you deeply enough to want to marry you. I quite understand why you're upset. Let's have lunch another time, Alex. I must get back to the bank.' She started for the door.

Diana's raised voice caught her. 'Oh, you're clever with words, aren't you? Well, let's see how you do with facts. Ryan only married you for your father's money, and he's not fool enough to divorce you till he's got some of it!'

Brittany stopped in mid-step, then forced herself to

keep walking. It was true enough, after all. Why should she be angry at Diana for having the gall to say what they all knew?

'Make sure that he gets the money,' Diana jibed, 'and then see how long he stays at the Castle!'

There was some comfort, Brittany thought, in knowing that Diana was wrong about that. Mere money, without the job he wanted, would never buy Ryan off. Or would it, despite what he had said?

How could I have been such a fool? she wondered. I should have known from the beginning that Ryan and I would never suit.

A milk-and-water miss, was she? And Ryan wanted someone with life, with spirit—someone like Diana.

The very idea made Brittany feel ill.

CHAPTER FIVE

BRITTANY stepped back and tipped her head critically, staring up at the twelve-foot tree. The sharp scent of pine needles fresh from the outdoor cold made her nose twitch. 'I think that's the best side,' she said at last. 'You can fasten it down in the holder now.'

Peters and the deliveryman seemed to heave a joint sigh of relief. As they finished securing the tree, Brittany turned toward the other end of the drawing room where Lydia was poking through boxes of ornaments.

'Look, Britt,' she said, 'here are the candleholders that your grandmother used on her tree. No electric lights for her! It was the old way or nothing, and she used candles till she died.'

Brittany picked up the metal holder and glanced from it to the tree. 'It's a wonder she didn't burn the house down,' she remarked.

'That's right. I remember being invited to her house on Christmas Eve, when your mother and I were small.'

'You always were best friends, weren't you?'

Lydia smiled. 'I can't remember a time when I didn't know Anne.' She turned the candleholder over and said thoughtfully, 'Your grandmother's tree was always in the front parlour, and we were never allowed to peek at it early. Then, after supper on Christmas Eve, she would light the candles for an hour or so, and that was all, till the next year.' She looked down at the stubby candle still in the holder. 'It seemed more special that way, somehow,' she said wistfully. 'Now it's so easy to have a glistening tree that we don't appreciate the light as much.'

'Sorry, Lydia. No candles.' Brittany picked up a string

of brightly coloured electric bulbs, tested them, and climbed up the ladder.

Lydia laughed. 'Did I sound as if I was hinting? I'm sorry; I didn't mean to. Only a fool would take chances with candles in a house like this.'

Brittany came down after another string of lights. 'But I can't agree with your notion that it's easy to have a modern tree. Do you know how many lights it takes to make a tree this size look nice?,

'Thousands, I suppose. Can I help?'

'Not with these. The tinsel is your department—I hate putting the stuff on.' She reached around a branch, and her bright plaid shirt came untucked from the waistband of her jeans. 'I'm just glad you came over to help.'

'When Clint said you were putting the tree up today all by yourself, I couldn't imagine it.' Lydia briskly sorted shimmering glass balls into a basket. 'Why, Brittany? You have enough household help—they could do it in an hour.'

'And it would look like it, too. I hate institutional trees—they have no personality.' She was behind the tree by then, and her voice was muffled. 'Mother and I always did it together, from the time I was big enough to help.'

Lydia laughed. 'And before that, too. I remember the year you were born. Anne put your bassinet beside the tree, and she sang carols to you while she hung the ornaments.'

'Perhaps that explains the fascination.'

'It might, at that.' Lydia's voice had grown soft. 'When are you going to carry on the tradition with a little one of your own, Britt?'

'Have a heart, Lydia!' Brittany hoped she sounded merely distracted, and not irritated. The mere mention of a baby brought longing to her heart. 'Ryan and I have only just decided to try marriage again.'

'I'm sorry.' There was a long silence. 'I think Clint

would love the idea.'

'I know he would. But I can't help thinking that if he's so fascinated by babies, he ought to get married again himself, instead of depending on me.'

Lydia sounded horrified. 'I can't imagine Clint ever doing such a thing! He loved Anne——'

'Of course he did. We all did.' Brittany looped the strand of lights around a branch. 'But we have to face facts, Lydia. Mother has been gone for more than a year, and he's terribly alone. She wouldn't have wanted him to be lonely.'

'Well, I can't imagine Anne would like the idea of Clint with a new family.' Lydia sounded a bit prim.

Brittany had to laugh. 'Well, perhaps not,' she conceded. 'But Mother had a sense of humour, and you must admit it would be funny to see Dad at a tiny tots' dance recital. Or a PTA meeting. Or in the paediatrician's office. He'd turn into a marshmallow over a new baby, and you know it.'

Lydia tried to smother a chuckle, and lost the battle. 'I see what you mean. Oh, look, here's a little spun glass angel! Isn't she pretty?'

Brittany looked over her shoulder. 'Mother brought me that from Venice when I was six.'

'Do you remember every one of these ornaments?'

'Almost.'

'Tell me about this one.' Lydia stretched out a hand. She held a cheap little bell, woven from straw and tied with a bright red ribbon. 'It's such a little thing—it must have a fascinating story.'

The sight of the little bell took Brittany back for a moment, to a noisy street market in Acapulco, where she had picked out the ornament in a moment of fancy and begged Ryan to buy it for her. He had haggled with the vendor and finally carried the trinket away in triumph, a souvenir of honeymoon joy. The little bell had got crushed in their luggage on the way home, and Brittany had salvaged and reshaped it and hung it on their first Christmas tree, here in this very room . . .

'I don't remember where that one came from,' she said. There was a note of finality in her voice, and Lydia put the ornament down suddenly, as if it had grown too hot to hold.

Christmas, Brittany thought. It had long been her favourite time of year, with friends stopping in and glittery parties and impulsive gift-buying. But this year——

For one thing, she had no idea what to give Ryan. It was clearly necessary to get him something; eyebrows would raise all over town if she didn't. But too much time had elapsed, and she no longer had any idea what he might want. She didn't want to give him any of the usual gifts from wife to husband. She could imagine the cynical gleam in his eyes if he were to open a package and pull out a new bathrobe, for instance. She could give him a wristwatch, but that seemed too impersonal. She could hardly give him anything for use around the house, for Ryan would not be at the Castle long.

Luggage? she thought, with a twinge of humour. It at least wouldn't give Ryan the idea that she wanted him to stay!

I don't want to spend Christmas morning alone with him, she thought. He's been here two weeks already, and I'm tired of the whole idea. It's such a sentimental time of year, such a family-orientated time. Why did Ryan have to mess up my holiday?

The gleam of an idea began to form in the back of her mind. If you don't want to be alone with him, she told herself, then have a party.

Last Christmas, with her mother so recently gone, had been a lonely one. She and Clint had rattled around the Castle, almost without words. They had opened gifts quietly, choked down a turkey dinner in almost total silence, spent the long hours watching television. They hadn't even had Lydia to break the silence last year; she had gone on a cruise.

'Are you staying in town for Christmas, or deserting us again?' asked Brittany.

'I'll be here. There was something about Christmas without snow that depressed me, so I thought I'd stay here and go south in January.'

'Great. Why don't you come and stay with us?'

Lydia looked startled. 'Brittany, I live less than six blocks away!'

'Who cares? Pretend it's a thousand miles. We'll have fun.'

'I always do, but—your first Christmas with Ryan? Are you certain you want me here to complicate things?'

Brittany gave her points for being perceptive. Then, with a quick smile, she said, 'Absolutely. You can entertain Dad.'

Lydia laughed. 'He's made a few noises to me about setting up his own home again.'

That's the last thing I need, Brittany thought. 'I hope he doesn't get into any hurry.' Of course, she added to herself, if he did, then Ryan could move out of her bedroom, and give them both a little peace!

'I think he feels he's intruding on the young lovers,' explained Lydia.

'In a ten-bedroom house, how can anyone intrude?' The last string of lights was on the tree. Brittany plugged them all in and stood back to admire the glistening multi-coloured bulbs.

'Are you sure you can handle a party at Christmas?' Lydia asked. 'On top of spending that weekend with the Governor and Mrs Curtis——'

'Now we can start on the ornaments,' said Brittany, and Lydia handed her the basket. 'I don't think I'm going. Cottages on the lake never appealed to me all that much. Especially in the winter.'

Lydia looked surprised. 'But Mrs Curtis is counting on you,' she said. 'She's so excited that you're coming, and she'd be devastated if you backed out.'

'And how do you know?'

'I ran into her at a tea yesterday. It was all she could talk about—the romance of it, and how you and Ryan were such a perfect couple.'

Brittany wanted to sit down and cry.

'That's the biggest tree I've ever seen,' a voice in the doorway observed.

Brittany turned. 'Hi, Jeff. Aren't you a little ahead of schedule today?'

Jeff pushed his glasses up on his nose. His cheeks were red from the outdoor cold. 'Ryan said he'd be home early. Can I use your computer to do my homework while I wait for him?'

Out of the corner of her eye, Brittany could see Lydia's eyebrows raising. 'Do you know how to run it?'

'Sure. We did it in school.'

'Well, be careful with it. It belongs to the bank, you know.' He rewarded her with a toothy smile and retreated to her sitting room.

Lydia hung the spun glass angel carefully on the tree and asked, 'Well, what gives?'

'Oh, he's just one of Ryan's refugees. It's the most amazing thing about that man,' Brittany reflected. 'His clients not only trust him—they almost adore him.'

Lydia nodded towards the sitting room. 'Are you telling me that child is a client?'

'No one has given me all the details,' said Brittany, 'but Jeff got himself into some kind of trouble at school, and Ryan pulled him through. Now——'

'Do you mean he never told you what kind of trouble it was?'

'No. It was confidential information.' It was fair enough, Brittany thought. Ryan had obviously not told Jeff the whole truth about her, either; Jeff thought theirs was a marriage made in heaven.

'And he's hanging about your house?'

'Come on, Lydia! Surely you can't suspect Jeff of anything underhanded. He's only a child. Anyway, with a face like that, he could hardly be a budding crook.'

Lydia shrugged and kept silent.

Brittany dismissed the notion. Of course Lydia was suspicious; she had been herself, before she had got to know Jeff a little better, and grown to trust him. Then, a little bemusedly, she realised that it wasn't a matter of trusting Jeff at all. It was Ryan that she trusted . . .

Interesting, she thought.

'I think I'll invite Dr Whittaker for Christmas, too,' she decided. 'I don't think she has any family around here. She has her little daughter, of course, but it would be a lonely holiday just for the two of them.'

'That sounds like the voice of experience,' commented Lydia.

'You have no idea how awful it was last year. Don't desert us again, Lydia—ever.'

Lydia said dryly, 'That's charming of you, Britt, but I'm afraid Clint might not want me hanging around all the time.'

Brittany picked up a glass ball, as iridescent and delicate as a soap bubble, and anchored it firmly on a branch. Then she turned to stare at Lydia.

The older woman turned a delicate shade of pink, and tried to hide her face in the basket of ornaments. 'I do try not to be a nuisance,' she said hesitantly.

'A nuisance? Lydia Stratman, how you could ever imagine yourself to be a nuisance——!'

'I'm afraid your father thinks of me that way sometimes,' Lydia said softly.

'But that's ridiculous! You saved his sanity there at first, by making him talk about Mother, instead of bottling up all that grief——'

'Yes,' Lydia said, with a sigh, 'I suppose that's true. And now whenever he sees me, I remind him of Anne, and what he's lost . . .'

Brittany stared at her for a long moment. 'I see.' She sat down in a wing-backed chair, and looked up at the other woman.

'She's all he talks about,' Lydia said. She brushed a hand across her eyes, and forced a brave smile to her lips.

'Oh!' Brittany exclaimed, on a long note of discovery. 'I think I begin to understand.' How could I have been so slow? she wondered. Lydia and Dad—— 'How long have you been in love with him?' she asked gently.

'Brittany, why on earth would you say a thing like that——' Then Lydia looked up, and her composure disappeared. When her eyes met Brittany's, she bit her lip and said, 'Years. Even before he married Anne.'

So that was why Lydia Stratman had never married. Brittany had wondered, now and then, why such a wonderful woman had remained single.

'I'm sorry I teased you about Dad starting a new family,' she said.

'Well, it would be understandable. A young wife wouldn't remind him so of Anne.' Lydia smiled. It didn't quite reach her eyes, but it was a courageous attempt. 'And if it would make him happy . . .' There was a long pause. 'We're not getting this tree decorated, Brittany. Get to work!'

The confiding moment was past, and Aunt Lydia was back—the woman who was always there, like a rock to lean on. Brittany wondered why she had never noticed before that Lydia, too, was vulnerable.

'It's a lovely dress.' Felice was almost ecstatic about the

cream and gold fabric that billowed out of the boutique box. 'And the gloves and the shoes and the handbag——'

'I didn't buy a handbag,' Brittany said.

'But there is one here, madam.' The maid handed over the gold leather bag in triumph.

'That sounds like Alexandra,' muttered Brittany. The girl never missed an opportunity to make a sale, but Brittany had to admit that the bag was the perfect finishing touch.

'Madam will wear it tonight?'

'No. It's only an ordinary dinner, Felice. Just the two of us.' Clint had gone to a club meeting that would last till all hours, so she and Ryan would be alone for the first evening since he had moved into the Castle.

Felice said wisely, 'And that makes it special enough, madam. You will want to look lovely for your husband, yes?'

Brittany almost said, No, but caught herself in time. Thank heaven, she thought, that Ryan wasn't there to hear the maid's remark. He had been in, changed to dinner clothes without a word to her, and left again, while Felice had been working on Brittany's hair. It had taken him less than ten minutes. Men were lucky, she thought rebelliously.

'Such a pretty dress,' Felice said again, touching the filmy fabric with a careful finger.

'Nevertheless, Felice, I'll save the new dress for the Foundation Christmas party this weekend.'

The maid looked brokenhearted. 'But Mrs Masters——'

'Don't argue with me, Felice,' Brittany warned, and realized that she had never made such a statement to her maid before. It's all Ryan's influence, she thought; a little of that sort of treatment and Felice had suddenly become an authority on everything! 'I'll wear my coffee-coloured dress, please.'

'Brown?' Felice muttered, irrepressibly, and fell silent under Brittany's warning glance.

But even Felice approved when, a few minutes later, Brittany was ready to go downstairs. The dress was the precise shade of mild coffee with a tiny bit of cream, and it emphasised the deep, rich brown of Brittany's hair and eyes. It was severely plain, high-necked and long-sleeved. But the top layer of fabric was chiffon, so nearly transparent that it did not hide Brittany's slender arms or her pretty shoulders. Under the chiffon was a slim-cut satin slip that rustled when she moved.

She fastened long gold earrings into her lobes and gave a final touch to her make-up. 'You needn't wait for me tonight, Felice.'

Felice gave her a pointed little smile. 'I should say *not*, madam,' she murmured, and bustled about the dressing room, picking up Brittany's discarded clothing. 'I'll be gone long before you and Mr Masters want your privacy.'

Brittany drew a breath to reply, but before she had decided what to say, Felice went on, 'I do hope he'll be careful with that dress—it's so delicate and all.'

Brittany clenched her teeth. Felice had opened a closet door and turned her back. Brittany fought down the longing to inform her maid curtly that Ryan would never lay a finger on that dress, that she was not dressing to please Ryan, and that she had no intention of needing her privacy, because the last thing she wanted on earth was for Ryan Masters to make love to her.

And besides all that, she thought, he wouldn't have to be told to be careful of her dress. Ryan always took very good care of clothing—his own, or hers. Brittany couldn't say the same for herself, she thought, a blush rising in her cheeks. Once, in the first months of their marriage, she had ripped the buttons off his shirt in her eagerness to be in his arms. He had scolded her for that later, she remembered, with a secret little smile, her eyes soft. But she hadn't cared about the scolding, for she had still been glowing from his lovemaking at the time ...

Felice turned back from the closet. 'Oh,' she said wisely, 'now I've embarrassed you. I'm sorry, madam.'

Brittany swallowed the sharp retort that trembled on her lips. Silly of her, to let a chance remark from her maid send her off on a silly merry-go-ground of how things used to be. And it would be sillier still to take out her frustration on the hapless maid.

'Wake me early in the morning,' she said, and swept down the hall to the marble stairway.

It was stupid of her, she decided, to care what Felice thought. What difference did it make if the maid thought Brittany was planning to seduce her husband tonight? If anything, it would help to promote the illusion among the staff that all was well in their marriage. Certainly that was better than the opposite. Servants did talk, after all, and——

'And the whole thing is ridiculous,' Brittany muttered to herself. 'You're beginning to sound like a broken record!'

Ryan was waiting for her in the drawing room. He was standing with one foot on a small stool, his elbow propped on his knee, staring at the Christmas tree. The glow from the thousands of tiny lights, magnified and reflected by the tinsel that Lydia had hung so carefully strand by strand, spilled over the Aubusson carpet and over Ryan.

What was he thinking? she wondered, as she came silently into the room. She had scarcely seen him in the last few days; he usually came home just minutes before dinner, and seldom came upstairs to their bed at night until she was asleep.

Did he plan it that way? she wondered, and felt a tiny flame of anger building inside her. As if she would want him to be there! Did he think she welcomed his presence in that big bed—that unless he stayed away, she might even try to persuade him to make love to her?

And what was he thinking of, as he stood there so quietly, unaware of her presence? Was it Diana Winslow who strolled through his thoughts tonight?

Her throat ached, just a little, with regret for what might have been. If things had happened just a little differently two years ago, they might have been upstairs now, in the nursery at the head of the stairway, tucking their baby in for the night, then coming down to share the little details of the day over dinner, and then going up to bed together——

And Ryan would still have been thinking of Diana Winslow, Brittany told herself harshly. Dreaming of what might have been didn't change things as they were, and she'd better not forget it.

She walked across the room and poured tomato juice into a glass. Ryan turned, and said half-heartedly, 'I didn't hear you come in. I would have got that for you.'

Brittany shrugged. 'I'd hate to put you to the trouble.'

His eyes darkened, but he didn't respond. He turned back to his inspection of the tree.

Brittany carried her glass across the room and sat down in a straight-backed chair. 'I'm surprised Jeff isn't still here,' she said.

'I sent him home.' He turned to look at her. 'You've been very kind, to let him spend so much time here.'

'I didn't realise I had a choice,' Brittany shrugged. 'Does it really bother you to have him hanging around?'

Surprisingly enough, she realised, it didn't. She shook her head. 'Though I'm surprised that his parents put up with it,' she said.

'They're relieved when he's not at home,' he said thoughtfully. 'Jeff's intelligence frightens them.'

'Oh? What keenly intelligent things got him into

trouble? And should I be frightened of him as well?'

Ryan laughed. 'Of Jeff? Of course not.'

Peters came down the shallow steps into the drawing room. 'Dinner is served, madam.'

In the dining room, Ryan held her chair. His hand lingered on her shoulder for a moment, as he looked thoughtfully down the long table, and finally Brittany looked up at him enquiringly, wondering what on earth was making him stand there so long.

'Don't you ever feel all this is just a little ridiculous?' he said finally.

Brittany looked down the length of the crisp linen tablecloth. Peters had left the room, and the only sound was the murmur of music from the concealed speakers. The only light in the room fell from the sconces along the side walls and the candles on the table—was that what Ryan was objecting to? She felt like telling him that the romantic atmosphere hadn't been her idea. Then she shrugged. 'I enjoy my home,' she said. 'Why on earth shouldn't I?'

Ryan pulled out his chair. 'The flowers, the candles, the silver, the formal clothes, for heaven's sake—just so two people can eat a meal?'

'I happen to like it this way,' she said, and picked up her seafood fork to sample the shrimp cocktail.

'It seems a terrible waste of resources.'

'I'm sure you'd prefer a hamburger in front of the fireplace,' she said tartly.

Ryan smiled. 'That would depend entirely on who I was sharing the hamburger with.'

'I assumed you'd be sharing it with a book,' snapped Brittany. 'And while we're speaking of formal clothes, don't forget that the Foundation Christmas party is Friday, and it requires white tie and tails.'

'May I remind you,' he returned coolly, 'that I've managed to show up, properly dressed, for the last two

years, without your assistance? Why should I have any
difficulty this year?'

She would have retorted, but Peters came in just then
to clear the first course, so she merely smiled down the
table at her husband and told herself that there might be
some advantages after all to his style of living. If they had
been eating hamburgers alone by the fire, she could have
thrown hers at him . . .

Peters brought in the main course. Brittany stared
down at beef Stroganoff and wondered how long she
would have to put up with living like this. The strain was
beginning to wear on her, the necessity of appearing
always calm when her nerves were stretched like rubber
bands. She had thought it would be easier tonight,
without her father there. But it wasn't. With Clint
present, somehow it was easier to play a part, to pretend
happiness.

As soon as Peters was gone, she asked abruptly, 'How
long are you going to be at the Castle, Ryan?'

He looked up, as if mildly interested. 'Why? Are you
anxious to be rid of me?'

'Do you need to ask?' Then she bit her tongue. 'I'm
serious, Ryan. I'd like to make some plans——'

'Plans that include Eric?' His tone was light, casual.

'Possibly. What business is it of yours?'

'None at all. Just a general interest.' It was hard to read
his expression in the dim room, but he sounded
unconcerned as he continued, 'The Governor plans to
announce all his staff appointments by the end of
January.'

Brittany tried to swallow her protest, but it came out as
a moan. 'That long?'

'I did warn you at the outset, Brittany.'

'I know—but it's been two weeks already and it feels
like forever. I had no idea it could last so long.'

'Your father thinks it may be sooner than that,

however.'

'What does he know about it?'

'Probably more than you think. He and Dan Curtis are very close, you know. And of course, there are things you could do to speed it up.'

'Like what?' she asked warily.

Ryan grinned. 'Don't jump to conclusions, Brittany. They're simple things, really—like going to the Curtises' lake cottage next weekend instead of finding an excuse to get out of it.'

'And you really think that will help?'

He shrugged. 'It shouldn't take me two days to convince the Governor I'd be a wonderful consumer advocate. Not when I have his full attention.'

Brittany sighed and remembered what Lydia had said about Mrs Curtis this afternoon. She wasn't about to tell Ryan; he would consider it just one more weapon to hold over her head. 'All right,' she said finally. 'I'll go.'

He didn't seem particularly pleased. Of course, she thought. He had known all along that she'd give in.

'And as soon as you get the job, we'll start the divorce,' she said firmly.

Ryan frowned. 'As soon as we can,' he said. 'We'll have to wait till I start to work. I'd hate to be fired before my first day on the job.'

'In that case,' said Brittany, 'I know I can't stand it that long!' She ate her beef Stroganoff in silence, but it didn't taste very good.

Just how long would it be, she wondered, before she was free? Would she have to wait till Ryan was established in this new job? And how long, she wondered, as panic began to rise inside her, was that going to take?

It was beginning to feel like forever.

CHAPTER SIX

'ARE you ready for these, madam?' Felice asked. She held out the shoulder-length gold kid gloves.

'Not quite, Felice.' Brittany was preoccupied with putting the final touches of mascara on her long lashes. More than that, she was preoccupied with her thoughts. They were due to arrive at the Foundation's Christmas party in less than an hour, and Ryan had not yet come home.

He's doing it on purpose, she thought. He wants to embarrass me.

For the last two years, since Ryan had left the Castle, her father had been her escort to this annual, glittery celebration of the holiday season. But this time, Clint had—at Brittany's gentle suggestion—decided to ask Lydia to act as hostess. When Brittany had first brought up the idea, Clint had smiled at her across the breakfast table and quickly agreed, assuming with delight that she had suggested it because she wanted to be with Ryan that night.

Well, whatever her father thought wasn't going to change her actions, Brittany told herself firmly. After all, it was to her advantage too to keep everyone believing that all was well at the Castle. The sooner Ryan was established in that new job, the sooner the farce would be over.

Or would it? Would that just be the beginning of a whole new round of blackmail? Would Ryan then be urging her to stay married, so he could preserve his job?

Her hand jerked nervously, and the mascara brush made a dark streak across her eyelid. She swore under her breath and reached for a cotton swab to remove it.

How could I have been such a fool? she thought. Of course! That's it; that's been what he was planning to do all along. Ryan doesn't want that job at all. He just wanted to re-establish himself here—in the Castle, with the prospects and the contacts, and the Bridges money. And I fell for his sad story of wanting a job. What a naïve, innocent little dummy you are, Brittany Masters! You kicked him out once, and now he's found a way to come back. All of a sudden he has the upper hand, and you're in his power——

She was amazed that he had drawn the line at seducing her. Surely sleeping with her would be little enough of a price for Ryan to pay for the advantages he sought, and it would have the advantage for him of keeping her off balance.

Bitterness rose in her. Was he simply not able to conceal his distaste now, as he had when their marriage was new? Then, he had enjoyed making love to her—at least, she remembered bitterly, he seemed to have enjoyed it. Now he avoided even the most casual touch, except when there was someone around who might be impressed by a show of affection.

He's taken advantage of me, she thought. And now he seems to have gone into hiding, so that I'll have to walk into the Foundation party by myself. Surely, though, he knows what kind of talk there will be. Surely he doesn't want that——

And who cares what he wants? Brittany asked herself. It's not the end of the world. If he isn't here in fifteen minutes, I'll go on. I won't wait around for him, and be even more embarrassed by missing the party altogether.

He would, no doubt, come home late with some excuse. He certainly would never admit to missing this affair on purpose. The excuse would be perfectly plausible, but whatever it was, Brittany didn't want to hear it.

Felice tucked a few cosmetics into the tiny gold handbag. 'Your mink is already downstairs,' she said. 'You do look lovely tonight, madam.'

Brittany murmured something vague and reached for her wedding ring. It, along with earrings, was the only jewellery she would wear tonight, the gloves, bag and shoes would provide all the glitter that was necessary. Other women at the party would be dripping diamonds, but Brittany rather enjoyed the idea of being different.

The ring felt heavy on her finger. She twisted it around, trying to make it more comfortable. Another six weeks at least of wearing it—she wasn't sure she could bear it; the memories it brought back were too strong.

'Don't worry, madam,' Felice said wisely, watching the nervously-twisted ring. 'He'll be here. No man in the world would pass up the chance to claim you as his wife tonight.'

Thanks anyway, Brittany almost said, but you obviously don't know Ryan Masters very well!

The sitting room door banged, and Ryan came in. 'Sorry to be late,' he said. 'Give me ten minutes and I'll be ready to go.'

Brittany closed her eyes and wondered why she seemed to be feeling relieved, instead of angry or frustrated.

What did I tell you? Felice's look said. 'Your clothes are laid out, sir,' she told him, and vanished into the bathroom to turn on the shower.

Ryan grinned. 'Lovely girl, isn't she?' he said.

Brittany gritted her teeth. So could we all be, she almost said, if we didn't have anything better to do than wait on a man hand and foot!

He stripped off his jacket and hung it in the closet. Brittany slipped her hand into one gold kid glove and carefully worked her fingers into the delicate leather, making sure her ring didn't tear the seam.

She wasn't aware that Ryan was watching her until he said, a little unsteadily, 'Did you know that little trick with the gloves looks almost as sexy as a striptease?'

Brittany looked up, startled, to find him very close beside her. His shirt was unbuttoned and he was removing his gold cufflinks. His bare chest looked warm and inviting, and she knew that if she laid her head against it, she would feel the strong beat of his heart under her ear.

And why would I want to do that? she asked herself fiercely.

His fingertips brushed against the leather at her wrist, then slipped to the bare skin on the inside of her arm where she had just started to fasten the tiny buttons. His touch was like fire, creeping up her arm.

So it's started, she thought. The seduction routine begins. He's finally decided that, to get what he wants, he needs to have me off balance, confused, begging for the physical satisfaction that he used to give me.

Well, he has a lot to learn, she told herself with determination.

Felice reappeared. 'You may go,' Brittany told her. The maid just grinned knowingly, bobbed a curtsy, and vanished. It made Brittany want to wring the girl's neck.

She felt almost sorry for him, she thought dispassionately. Poor Ryan—thinking that all he had to do was to touch her, and she'd melt in his arms again. How foolish of him!

'If I'd known you had a glove fetish,' she said sharply, 'I'd have stopped wearing them years ago.' She picked up the other glove and her handbag, and started for the door.

The barb glanced off Ryan. He took his shirt off and smiled across the room at her. 'That, my dear Brittany, is why I never told you before,' he said. 'And I wouldn't have said it tonight, except that I was overcome by your charms.'

She paused in the doorway. 'I do hope, for your sake, that Felice made that a cold shower,' she said tartly.

His mocking laugh followed her down the hall.

It was very little more than ten minutes later when he came down the stairs, every hair in place, the white tie perfect, the white waistcoat spotless, the black tailcoat brushed and well-fitting.

Brittany was in the sitting room, watching over Jeff's shoulder as he manoeuvred pie-shaped pieces of a graph around on the screen of her computer and turned them various colours.

'Do you like blue?' he asked. 'I'll change them all to shades of blue if you want.'

'I had no idea the computer would do that,' she said.

Jeff looked bitterly disappointed in her. 'What do you use it for, anyway?' he asked.

'Mostly just to call the bank and see what kind of customer a client is,' she admitted. 'The idea was to put it here so I could work at home, but I don't do that often. Jeff, I think you're a genius!'

Ryan said, 'Absolutely right, Brittany.' His tone was cool. 'And that's where we get into trouble.'

Jeff looked up at him, eyes wide and almost panicky.

'You promised, Jeff,' Ryan told him flatly.

'I'm not doing anything, Ryan—really,' the child insisted. 'And I didn't promise never to touch a computer again. I only said I——'

'See that you remember,' Ryan told him. 'It seems to me that it's past time for you to go home.'

'Yes, sir,' said Jeff regretfully. He punched a combination of commands and the brilliant pie-graph disappeared from the screen.

Brittany was looking back and forth between the two intense faces. 'What was that all about?' she asked as Ryan reached for her arm.

'I see you put on the other glove without waiting for me,' he remarked.

'Too bad you missed the show!'

'That's all right. You'll have to take them off some time.'

And it will be when you aren't around, she thought, if I have to wait till tomorrow morning!

Ryan took her mink from Peters and possessively helped her into it, his fingers lingering longer than necessary at the nape of her neck.

We're going to have to put an end to this, Brittany thought. And soon—very, very soon.

The Rolls was waiting at the front door. As soon as it pulled out into the street, Brittany determinedly moved away from Ryan on the seat and said, 'I think I should know what all that was about——'

He shrugged. 'I happen to like women in gloves.'

'Not that,' she said, fighting down a blush. 'I meant the business with Jeff and the computer. You weren't pleased to see him using it, that was plain. I think I have a right to know.'

He was silent for a few moments. 'He was nearly expelled from school last year for selling grades.'

'Selling—how?'

'According to Jeff, it was ridiculously simple. He was calling up the school's computer, giving the password, and breaking into the records, where he altered a grade here and there.'

'For a fee, of course.'

'Actually, he only did it for friends.'

'Well!' Brittany was silent for a moment. 'Perhaps I should lock up the computer.'

Ryan shrugged. 'He promised never to experiment

again. But if I were you, I wouldn't leave my password lying around. The school didn't press charges, but I'd hate to have to defend him against First Federal.'

'Do you realize the amount of damage he could do?'

'Oh, quite.'

Brittany was thinking about how easily Jeff had manoeuvred the pie-graph. If he were to get into the bank's records——

But that's impossible, she told herself. The security system wouldn't allow a novice to break in. And Jeff couldn't possibly have the necessary expertise. 'He's only a child,' she said.

Ryan was watching the emotions play across her face. 'That's where you're wrong, you know,' he said. 'The kids are the ones who are dangerous. They aren't bogged down in logical thinking, so they can take all kinds of new creative paths. And Jeff is quite good—that's why he wasn't expelled, actually. They'd have loved to, but they couldn't prove that he wasn't making passing grades!'

She shivered and pulled the mink collar close around her neck. 'You could have told me, Ryan.'

'I didn't know you had the darn thing. The desk has been closed every time I've been in that room.'

'I seldom use the computer.'

'I'm amazed. Having it right there in the house would make a good excuse to work twenty-four hours a day instead of only fifteen.'

'I wouldn't throw stones if I were you, Ryan. It seems to me you spend plenty of time at that legal clinic.' Unless, she realised, he hadn't been at the clinic tonight at all. He might have been anywhere—with Diana Winslow, for instance. She bit her lip.

Ryan shrugged. 'People don't arrange to have their legal problems happen at my convenience,' he said.

There seemed to be no answer to that, so Brittany said

nothing. The Rolls pulled up at the main entrance of the city's most elegant hotel, and the doorman helped them out. Ryan's hand went possessively to Brittany's elbow, and she had to fight down the instinct to shake him off.

What had caused this? she wondered. He had scarcely touched her for days; now he seemed unwilling to let her out of arm's reach.

Then she answered her own question. This was the first big social function of his return, and he wasn't going to let anyone get the wrong idea.

I'll just put up with it tonight, she told herself wearily. And when we get home, I'll shred him, and he'll never dare touch me again!

It had been Brittany's mother's idea to make the Foundation Christmas ball the most formal occasion in the city. Now it had become tradition for the arrivals' names to be announced at the door of the Grand Ballroom by a gentleman whom Brittany suspected of being a former Marine Corps sergeant.

Nevertheless, she told herself, real social standing in this city was to be recognised at the door of the Foundation ball, without having to whisper your name in the announcer's ear.

'Mr and Mrs Ryan Masters!' the announcer bellowed, and Brittany put her fingertips lightly on Ryan's arm and descended the shallow steps into the ballroom.

Alexandra Warren was the first to greet her. She was wearing improbable lilac that looked wonderful with her red hair upswept, and a diamond bracelet glittered on her wrist. 'Don't you look gorgeous tonight,' she murmured to Ryan. 'And darling—that dress is superb on you.'

Brittany laughed. 'I bet you tell that to all the girls,' she returned. 'You probably sold most of the dresses that are here tonight.'

'Oh, a good third of them.' Alex was undisturbed by the accusation. 'But not many of them are carried off with your kind of style. No jewellery? I must admit, I visualised that dress with pearls—but I think you're right after all. Pearls would have been just a little too— virginal.' She flashed a smile. 'I must be off to say hello to the rest of my ladies.'

Virginal! Brittany thought.

'We should greet your father,' murmured Ryan.

'By all means,' she snapped, through a sweet smile. 'Do make sure that we don't miss any of the proprieties, darling.'

His hand tightened painfully on her arm, and Brittany was obscurely pleased. So it was possible to irritate Ryan, was it? His skin wasn't quite as thick as he pretended.

Clint and Lydia were standing on a little platform off to the side of the ballroom, with the chairman of the Foundation's board of directors and his wife. Last year Brittany had been on that platform beside her father, greeting the hundreds of guests. She found that she didn't miss it at all.

Clint gave her a careful hug. 'You're late, Miss Britt,' he accused. 'Taking advantage of the fact that I released you from official duties, hmm?'

Brittany laughed and gave Lydia a kiss. She looked radiant, Brittany thought, in pale pink. 'I'm glad you told me to wear comfortable shoes,' smiled Lydia.

'Experience,' Brittany returned briefly. 'Hello, Mr Chairman,' she said, turning to the white-haired man beside Lydia.

He looked from her to Ryan, who was giving Lydia an enthusiastic hug. 'Well, I knew there was something in the wind at the last meeting, when you two battled it out in the boardroom,' he told her. 'But I wouldn't have expected this.'

And you don't know the half of it, Brittany thought. She escaped from the receiving line with a sigh of relief.

The chamber orchestra was in its place on another

platform. Good, Brittany thought. At least when the
dancing starts I can avoid Ryan.

'They're going to play a couple of pieces by that new
composer we're funding,' he said.

'Whose bright idea was that? If I wanted a symphony
concert—'

'Your father's,' Ryan pointed out.

'In that case . . .' Brittany's eyes narrowed as she
studied the platform. 'There are instruments there I've
never seen before.'

'Not surprising. If you'd pay attention at board
meetings, you'd know that the composer also manufac-
tures new kinds of instruments.'

'I beg your pardon, but if a standard orchestra was
good enough for Beethoven——'

She broke off as Clint stepped up to a microphone.
'Tonight we have a special treat,' he announced. 'One of
the Foundation's new young artists has been persuaded
to come and share with us the world premiere of his new
style of music. I am pleased to present to you——'

Brittany snorted. 'Persuaded, my eye teeth!' she
muttered. 'He's probably been politicking for this
opportunity for a year.'

'Shh!' ordered Ryan. 'Don't you realize the Foundation holds a share in the patent rights on his new
instruments? If they were to take off in the market——'

'They'd be airplanes,' Brittany returned sweetly. 'And
they'd probably make a nicer sound.'

'Don't be a spoilsport. How would you have liked to
hold half the patent rights on the piano?'

'That, my dear Ryan, was a totally different thing.' She
turned her back on him to give full attention to the music.

The composer was young, wild-eyed and long-haired.
After the first few notes, Brittany winced and tried to
concentrate instead on the flaws in the young man's
tailoring; his formal clothes had obviously been rented

from the lowest bidder.

When polite applause had given way to blessed silence, she turned to Ryan with an ironically raised eybrow.

'He's only getting started,' he explained.

'Perhaps he could try creating an electric oboe next,' she suggested. 'That should have great possibilities.'

'These things take time. I wouldn't be surprised if he's a huge success some day.'

Brittany smiled nastily. 'Oh, that piece has real possibilities,' she said. 'Who knows—it might end up in a stomach-acid commercial. Illustrating the symptoms.'

Clint was back at the microphone. 'I'm sure you all enjoyed that just as much as I did,' he began, and Brittany choked on a giggle. 'A little later tonight we'll have some other performers who have received Foundation support. And we want to remind you that it's only through your generosity that these programmes are possible.'

'That was a bad miscalculation, Dad,' muttered Brittany. 'After that atrocity, you'll be lucky to scrape up ten bucks here tonight!'

'Without your gifts,' Clint continued, 'a whole generation of technical innovations would be lost. So when our canvassers ask you tonight for a generous donation, think hard—and then think big. Now I'll stop yammering and we'll get to the real business of the evening—the dancing!'

Brittany listened to the orchestra for a moment, and then sighed in relief. 'I don't believe it,' she said. 'I actually recognise the melody!'

'Braggart,' Ryan said softly, and put his arms around her. 'Shall we dance?'

'Do I have a choice?' The music was slow and dreamy, and it was the closest she had been to Ryan since he had come back to the Castle. She tried to hold herself stiffly away from him, but after a couple of minutes she reluctantly relaxed in his arms. There was no point in making a public fuss of it, after all.

He slanted a look down at her and said, 'Thank you. That was a little like dancing with a board.'

She ignored the jab. 'I'm amazed that people put up with this,' she said. 'They pay a healthy price for tickets, and then are subjected to things like that new composer.'

'And on top of it all they're hit up for another donation,' Ryan added.

'Oh, I don't think they care about that. Everyone here knows that for every dollar they give, Daddy adds another ten.'

'True. I'm amazed you don't mind.'

'Why should I?'

'Because it's your inheritance he's spending.'

And Ryan would rather be able to spend it himself . . . She bit her tongue to keep from saying the obvious. 'I'm tired of dancing,' she said.

'Very well.' They circled the room, on their way back toward their table. One of the red-coated canvassers smiled at Brittany.

'Can we rely on you for a donation, Mrs Masters?'

She shrugged and smiled. 'Of course, but I'm afraid that I didn't bring my chequebook tonight.'

'Oh, there are more ways to donate than by giving cold cash, Mrs Masters. Miss Warren just gave me this for the cause.' He held up Alex's diamond bracelet.

'Interesting,' commented Ryan.

'I noticed that earlier. I've never seen her wear it before,' said Brittany. 'I wonder if she planned to give it away.'

Ryan's eyes met hers with understanding. 'A memento of a long-gone man, and she doesn't want it around to remind her any more?,

'It's more likely that Alex bought it wholesale and is going to claim when she files her income tax that it was worth a mint.'

'You're a suspicious little creature!'

'Didn't you know? Bankers always are.' She turned back to the canvasser. 'As far as I'm concerned, you're even out of luck on the jewellery. I'm not wearing any.'

He grinned. 'Better luck next time,' he said, and went on to the next table.

'Brittany,' said a hesitant voice beside her, 'will you come and dance with me?'

She saw Ryan's jaw set and his eyes harden even before she turned to look up at Eric Rhodes. 'Of course,' she said sweetly. 'Do excuse me, dear.' She patted Ryan fondly on the shoulder and rose.

Eric had swept her out on the floor before Ryan could say anything. Just as well, Brittany thought. Knowing that Ryan was still watching them, she gave Eric a brilliant smile. 'I've missed you lately,' she said. 'The way you've been hiding out in your office——'

He groaned. 'Don't remind me! I'm having to retrace the whole computer system, step by step, when I'd much rather be holding you.' His arms tightened a little.

Brittany concealed a sigh. 'Have you found the problem?'

'No. I can't find a hint anywhere.'

'But the clerk still insists that something is wrong?'

'Frankly, I'm beginning to suspect that she's creating the mix-up herself—to draw attention. She's certainly getting that,' he added with a rueful laugh. 'Everybody all the way up the ladder is getting involved.'

'What does Dr Whittaker say?'

Eric snorted. 'That nothing's wrong—when it's as obvious as the nose on your face that the woman needs a psychiatrist.' He drew her another inch closer. 'Not that there's anything wrong with your nose,' he added softly.

'As a matter of fact, it's a lovely little nose, and I've missed——'

'Eric!' she said warningly.

'Brittany, I'm getting desperate,' he said, and there was no denying the frantic note in his voice. 'I can't stand being without you——'

They had been edging closer to the wall, and now, with a quick glance around, he swept her through a small door into an alcove. 'I want you so much that it hurts me to see him touch you.'

It was rather nice, Brittany thought, to be wanted so desperately. A few weeks of living with an ice cube did dreadful things to a woman's self-image. But Eric still thought she was attractive——

She looked up at him with a smile, and he took it as encouragement. It was a hot, hasty kiss, ravaging, bruising in its intensity, a little frightening. 'Eric, please——' she protested.

'Does that mean you want him to go on?' a cool voice asked from the doorway.

Brittany looked up in horror to see Ryan standing there, leaning against the wall, arms folded across his chest, a casual and unconcerned observer.

Eric stepped in front of Brittany. 'I think it's time you knew the truth, Masters,' he said. 'Brittany and I love each other. I don't know how you managed to talk her into taking you back, but as soon as she'd done it, she knew it was a mistake. We're going to be married, and there's nothing you can do to stop us!'

'Eric——' This had got entirely out of hand, Brittany thought.

Ryan ignored her. A faint smile hovered on his lips. 'I know all about you, Eric,' he said softly. 'Brittany told me the whole story.'

'Then you know you have to let her go,' Eric said triumphantly.

'It was—quite amusing, actually. But you seem to misunderstand the situation. I'm not holding Brittany captive. She's quite free to do as she likes. And since she hasn't filed for a divorce, it seems to me it's because she doesn't want to. Perhaps you should take the hint, and give up.'

Oh, he was clever, Brittany thought bitterly. No wonder his clients worshipped him! He could take the truth and give it a mild twist and somehow it all came out looking different—looking sordid, somehow.

'I quite admit,' Ryan went on, casually, 'that I have an advantage. I suppose you think it would be sporting of me to move out of our bedroom while she makes up her mind—but you see, Rhodes, she's already decided.' He moved, just a little, and suddenly the casual stance became threatening. 'So go away. Now.'

Eric's upper lip curled just a little, then he looked down at her, and his expression softened, though there was still a wary look in his eyes. 'Brittany——'

'Please go, Eric. I'll talk to you later.'

He hesitated, then submitted. 'All right, because you ask it. But tell Tarzan there that he didn't make me do anything!' He stalked out of the alcove.

Brittany tossed her head and followed him. Ryan had resumed his casual position beside the door, and she didn't even see him move from it. But suddenly he was blocking her path, and his hands were firm on her upper arms.

'I'm so sorry I interrupted your recreation,' he said softly. 'It would have been polite of me to wait another few minutes—but then I'm not sure what I'd have walked in on.'

One quick move jerked her off balance, and she found herself leaning against him, her breasts pressing against his white waistcoat with every shallow breath she drew. 'It was only a kiss,' she said raggedly.

He raised an eyebrow. 'Only a kiss?' he said thoughtfully. 'But what kind of kiss? Was it like this?'

I suppose I deserve this, Brittany thought. He has some right to be angry; I did agree to put a civilised front on our marriage, and even though I didn't plan that little episode, I participated. I'll just wait Ryan out, and after he's tried every trick he knows, and I've laughed at him, he'll never dare to touch me again.

His mouth was cool and firm against her cheek. 'Oh, but it wasn't that kind of a kiss at all, was it?' he drawled.

She made a sudden convulsive attempt to escape, and his arms tightened around her like a straitjacket.

She looked up at him pleadingly. His eyes were so dark they were almost black, and he stared down at her for a few seconds as if debating with himself. Then he muttered something she couldn't hear, and his mouth came down on hers with punishing intensity.

If Eric's demanding kiss had been faintly frightening, this assault was terrifying. But it was not his actions that horrified her, Brittany realised, but her own response. She sagged in his arms like a puppet whose strings were broken and tangled. When his hand found the curve of her hip, pressing the whole length of her body against his, she didn't struggle. The sensation of heat broke over her in a wave, and all she could think of was how to put out the fire that raged deep inside her, threatening to send her mad.

The taste of him as his mouth probed hers was a remembered ecstasy; the feel of his hands turned the gauzy fabric of her dress into a barrier, a prison that she felt she must escape. It was as though she no longer had control of her own mind, as if Ryan's mere touch was destroying her free will and making her some kind of mindless zombie who had only the power to do as he demanded.

And then he pulled back from her, holding her upright

at arm's length until she had recovered her balance.

'Why?' she demanded, in a hoarse whisper, and didn't know herself if she was asking why he had kissed her like that, or why he had stopped.

'Poor Eric,' said Ryan. His voice was light, casual, but there was a rough edge to it, and his breathing was a little unsteady. 'He has no idea what he missed.'

Brittany's common sense was returning, and with it the knowledge that this time she had made a prime fool of herself. Anger began to bubble to the surface. 'Get out!' she ordered.

He bowed, as graceful as a king's courtier. 'You'd better do something with your hair,' he added. 'It's a little mussed, I'm afraid.' And he was gone, letting the door drop shut silently behind him.

CHAPTER SEVEN

BRITTANY clenched her fists till her nails cut caverns in her palms. How could she have submitted to that kind of treatment? she asked herself. How could she have simply stood there in Ryan's arms and allowed him to make her feel cheap? Why hadn't she kicked him, or clawed his handsome face, or screamed, or done something——

'I will not cry,' she said, in a low, hard voice. 'I will not give him the satisfaction of making me cry.'

Instinctively she smoothed her hair, trying to get it back into the twist that Felice had produced so carefully. It was difficult, with her sense of touch masked by the kid gloves. Irritably she tugged them off and with trembling fingers repaired her hair. It would get her by, she thought, and hoped she could make some excuse for leaving early.

Early, and without Ryan, she thought. She crammed the gloves into her tiny evening bag, heedless of the wrinkles and folds, and started back across the ballroom.

Alexandra Warren was sitting at the table they had shared earlier, sipping champagne, when Brittany sank into her chair.

'Where's Ryan?' asked Brittany.

Alex raised an enquiring eyebrow. 'Dancing. Why are you out of breath?'

'Alex, there are some questions that even a friend shouldn't ask! Would you be a pet and tell him I went on home?'

'Tell him yourself,' shrugged Alex, and gestured towards the dancers.

Brittany swung round in her chair. Within a dozen feet

106

of her, on the edge of the dance floor, was Ryan, and in his arms was Diana Winslow. It was a slow number, and the blonde was dancing so close to him that her deep-purple dress, Brittany thought, would probably have the imprint of his waistcoat buttons left on it when the dance was over.

He looked up, and caught her eyes. Two can play at this game, he seemed to be saying.

But she knew that Ryan was wise enough to keep his flirtation with Diana out in the open, where only Brittany would know what it meant. So far as the rest of the world knew, they were only dancing. On the other hand, if her escapade with Eric in the alcove was to become public, she would be condemned.

He's manoeuvred me into a corner again, she thought, and her fingers tapped on the tabletop in frustration. 'Nevertheless,' she told Alex, without taking her eyes off Ryan, 'I'd appreciate it if you gave him a message.'

But on the dance floor, Ryan had said something into Diana's ear, and they were coming towards the table. Brittany shivered and turned away with a little shrug. Her fingers clenched together, and the heavy wedding ring cut into her skin. She looked down at it. The star sapphire seemed to mock her, and the diamonds glittered coldly under the chandeliers.

One of the red-coated canvassers came over to them. 'Everybody's heard about your gift, Miss Warren,' he said with a smile. 'Mrs Masters? We can count on you, can't we?'

'I told the other man; I didn't bring my——' She paused and met Ryan's eyes as he came up to the table. Diana was clutching his arm. 'Here,' Brittany said softly, and wrenched the wedding ring from her finger. 'That's a seven-carat star sapphire. It should bring a pretty penny for the Foundation.'

The man was dumbfounded. 'Mrs Masters, I didn't

mean—Please—I'm sure you can't intend to give up your wedding ring!'

Brittany dropped the ring into his basket without a second look. 'Oh, yes, I do,' she said, and raised her eyes to meet Ryan's.

Our reconciliation is over, her steady gaze was saying, but Ryan didn't seem to see. He merely smiled. 'I'm sure they'll hold it for a day or two, Brittany, so you can reclaim it with a donation——'

'I won't change my mind,' she said firmly. 'I'm not feeling very well, Ryan. I think I'll go on home.'

She didn't see him move, and yet suddenly Diana's hand was no longer on his arm, and he was beside Brittany. 'I'll take you, of course.'

She should have expected that, she realised. No devoted husband would stay at a party if his wife was feeling ill. Certainly not Ryan. Brittany shook her head. 'There's no need. I'll be quite all right——' She was beginning to babble, she realised.

Ryan shook his head. 'Oh, I couldn't possibly allow you to go home alone if you're not well.'

'I don't want you,' she muttered under her breath.

He smiled coolly. 'I'm afraid you're stuck with me. I have the claim ticket for your coat.'

'You could just give it to me.'

Ryan ignored her. 'Put your gloves on, dear. We don't want you to catch cold. Goodnight, Diana—Alex.' With a nod, he drew Brittany's hand into the crook of his arm and started towards the main door.

'I don't want you to come with me!' she hissed.

He said mildly, 'I don't recall asking you if you wanted me.' He claimed her mink, helped her into it, glanced at her bare hands and raised an eyebrow.

'I wouldn't put those gloves on again if you got down on your knees and begged!' she snapped.

'Good. Then I won't beg.' They waited in silence for

the Rolls. When it pulled up under the portico, Ryan reached for her arm; Brittany pulled away from him with an artistic shudder. She climbed into the car and settled herself as far away from him as possible.

'I'm sure you're enjoying yourself,' he said, 'by pretending to be the violated heroine, but the fact is that I found you and your lover——'

'He is not my lover!'

'It certainly looked that way to me. I found the two of you together and merely handed out a bit of discipline to an erring wife.'

'An erring . . .! My God, Ryan, you sound positively medieval!'

'You might remember that,' he recommended. 'Not even your father would have objected. In fact, if he'd been the one to find you, you would probably have been spanked.'

'On the whole, I'd have preferred it!' Brittany settled herself with a flounce. 'One would think, from the way you talk, that you were jealous!,

A street light lit the car briefly, and Brittany saw his jaw set. He laughed, but it was without humour. 'I'm not jealous,' he said; his voice was low and taut. 'Don't flatter yourself, Brittany. You're beautiful as the very sirens themselves, but underneath—It doesn't take much time for a man to get tired of a spoiled little bitch who only cares about herself. Eric can have you, and welcome, just as soon as I get the job I want.'

Brittany's eyes stung with tears. How bitterly unhappy he was, she thought, to be saying these things to her.

'But in the meantime, my darling,' he went on, with heavy emphasis on the endearment, 'you will behave like a wife.'

She caught her breath in panic. What did he mean?

'In public,' he added harshly. 'Which is all I care about.'

The Rolls pulled up to the front door of the Castle. How much of that had the chauffeur heard? Brittany wondered. She clutched her collar around her throat and didn't look at Ryan as he held the door for her.

The staff had gone to bed. Brittany flung her coat across a chair in the hallway and stormed up the stairs.

Ryan caught her at the door of their suite. 'If you intend to lock me out,' he said darkly, 'let me warn you that you won't succeed.'

He followed her into the sitting room. Brittany picked up a hand-painted porcelain vase and threw it at him. Ryan ducked, and the vase splintered against the panelled wall, with water, roses, and porcelain fragments raining down on to the carpet.

There was an instant of shocked silence in the room, then Brittany shrugged. Her anger was suddenly gone, replaced by a heavy tiredness. Ryan bent to inspect the damage.

'Never mind,' she sighed. 'It's not important. Felice will clean it up in the morning.'

He straightened slowly and looked at her with an expression she had never seen before. His eyes were murderously bright, and as he took a step towards her, Brittany instinctively backed away.

'Felice wasn't the one who broke it,' he said between his teeth. 'It isn't going to wait till morning. You're going to clean it up, right now.'

She laughed uncertainly. 'Why do you think I have a maid?' she asked. 'I don't even know where the cleaning things are——'

'Then it's about time you learned,' he growled. 'In the meantime, you can use a towel.'

'How silly, Ryan—I'd have to change first.' She turned away, shrugging her shoulders.

His hand tightened on her arm, yanking her around to face him. 'Why?' he asked. 'You broke it wearing that dress. You can clean it up the same way.'

She was so close to him by then that she could feel his breath on her face. Her arm hurt. 'All right, you bully!' she snapped, and pulled away from him. She rubbed resentfully at the red spot his hand had made, then she knelt beside the shattered vase and began to pick up the pieces.

Ryan stood there like an avenging angel until each sliver of porcelain had been dropped into the wastebasket. He handed her a towel then, and watched as she mopped the water off the wall and squeezed it from the carpet. 'There,' she said at last, sitting back on her heels. 'Are you satisfied?'

'I'm sure you're incapable of doing better.' There was a moment's silence, then he said, 'I feel sorry for you, Brittany.'

'I'm honoured!' Her voice had a sarcastic edge.

'This is what happens to a person who has too much,' he said thoughtfully. 'Because you were always given everything, you never learned to appreciate anything. You knew when you were a baby that if you broke your toys, there would always be more.'

'Look, Ryan, I don't need this psychoanalysis tonight!'

'Now that you're older, people get in your way, and you break them too, because to you they're just like toys——'

'I don't have to listen to this!' She stood up.

'No. And you don't want to, because it's true. All your life, people have told you that you're beautiful. No one has ever dared to suggest to you, Brittany, that you might not be quite as beautiful on the inside.'

She turned towards the door.

'What would you do, Brittany, if you didn't have enough money to buy loyalty? If you couldn't pay Felice's wages, how long do you think she would put up with your tantrums?'

'She should be glad——' Brittany bit the sentence off.

'Oh, yes,' said Ryan coldly. 'She has so much here. A mistress who treats her like a dog, and——'

'Shut up!' Brittany put her hands over her ears. 'That's not true!'

'What do you know about her, Brittany? Do you know what she thinks, what she wants, what she dreams about? No—and you don't care, any more than you'd care about what a lapdog thought! Just remember, my dear, that inner beauty is the only kind that counts—the only kind that lasts.' Ryan stripped off his tail coat and started to unbutton his waistcoat. 'Some day, Brittany, something is going to hurt you badly enough to make you into a real woman, instead of a plastic doll. I thought perhaps losing the baby would make you see that you're not above ordinary human pain just because you have money——'

'Don't talk to me about the baby!' Her voice was harsh and low. How dared he! she thought.

He paused, and looked at her curiously. 'Why not? It was my baby too.'

'You didn't care.'

'Is that what you think? That baby was our only hope——'

'Your only hope, you mean! And I don't intend to talk about it any more!'

Ryan shrugged. 'Very well. Before you get any notions of murdering me in my sleep——'

'Don't tempt me!' Brittany flashed. 'But don't worry, I wouldn't come near you tonight if the alternative was to sleep out under the trees!' She slammed the door behind her and retreated down the stairs.

I'd stay up all night, she told herself, before I'd share a bedroom with him!

She stalked over to the cabinet that concealed the bar and started to pour herself a drink. Scotch splashed over the rim of the glass and on to the table. Then she realised that alcohol was the last thing she wanted, and reached for the bell instead. Peters would come and fix her a cup of tea——

She stopped herself before her finger hit the button, and pensively went to her sitting room, where she curled up on the windowseat and looked out over the lawn. She told herself that she'd merely changed her mind, but she was uneasily aware that it wasn't quite the truth. She was just a little afraid of what Ryan would say if she woke Peters to fetch her tea . . .

The cold, crisp air was like crystal outside. Moonlight lay across the frozen snow like melted butter. Brittany looked at it, but she didn't see it.

'Inner beauty is the only kind that lasts,' she murmured, repeating what Ryan had said. Was he right? Was she nothing but a spoiled, proud child who expected everyone and everything to bend to her wishes?

She had always had a nurse, a nanny, a maid, following her around. She couldn't remember the last time she had hung up a dress; Felice was always there to take it from her, or to pick it up from the back of a chair the next morning. It was Felice who dealt with the creases and wrinkles, with never a protest.

'And she's well paid for it, too,' Brittany muttered. Ryan didn't know what he was talking about.

Clint's key clicked in the front door. Brittany sat very still, hoping that he wouldn't look in. She didn't want to try to explain why she was sitting here alone in the dark.

But he went on upstairs, and she sighed in relief. He was very late. Had he stopped at Lydia's for a while? She hoped so. He was so lonely, and Lydia would be good for him. Perhaps they would even marry, eventually.

Be honest, she told herself. If Lydia had confessed her love for Clint a few months ago, Brittany would have been shocked and even hurt at the idea of her father leaving her. She would have thought of herself first.

It sobered her. Perhaps Ryan was right after all. He seemed to have the secret, at any rate. There were certainly enough people hanging around him, for no reason at all except sheer loyalty. Jeff, for example.

She rubbed her finger where the sapphire ring had rested, and thought about Ryan. There was a magnetism about him, something that drew people.

Not least of all, her. Her cheeks were hot in the darkness as she thought about how she had clung to him, there in the alcove off the ballroom tonight, how she had trembled in his arms, and responded to that fierce, demanding kiss, and wanted more——

'You weren't angry because he kissed you,' she told herself, 'but because he left you.'

How many times in the last two weeks, she thought, had she wondered why he had made no move towards her? She had thought then that she wanted him to make some attempt to seduce her, so that she could crush his pretensions with a cold rebuff, and make him feel like the worm he was.

Now she knew better. Tonight he had kissed her, and she had wanted him to do much more than that. The stabbing pain she had felt when she saw Diana Winslow in his arms had not been irritation, or anger at being beaten at her own game; it had been cold, hard jealousy that it was Diana in his arms, and not herself.

The bitter truth was that she still wanted him.

She put her forehead against the cold pane of glass. Her head ached, and she wanted to cry.

She sat there for a long time, then she crept up the stairs and into the master suite. She owed him an apology, she thought. She was spoiled, and thoughtless— he was right about that. 'But I'm not cruel, and I'm not heartless,' she told herself.

His breathing was deep and regular, and when she

softly called his name, he didn't answer. She stood there
in the darkness of the bedroom for a few minutes.

Bitterness rose to choke her. It mattered so little to
him, what he had said, that it hadn't even interfered with
his sleep! She might have been a client who needed a
dose of the truth, and not his wife.

Felice found her on the couch in the sitting room, still
wearing the crumpled cream-coloured dress, in the
morning.

Brittany came awake slowly, stretched, and uttered a
painful little moan as she realised how many sore places
there were on her body.

'Madam, you didn't sleep on the couch all night?'
Felice sounded horrified.

Brittany looked up at the maid. Felice's eyes were
puffy this morning, she thought idly. 'I'm sorry,' she said,
standing up and trying to shake out the dress. 'I didn't
think . . .'

'That's just it,' came a voice from the doorway. 'You
never think about anything but yourself.'

She didn't even turn towards him. What point was
there in trying to talk to him? she thought. What he
believed was too near the truth for her to deny it.

She stepped out of the dress, handed it to Felice,
wrapped herself in a satin robe, and sat down in front of
the dressing table.

There was a tap on the door. Felice went to answer it,
and came back to say, in a strangled whisper, 'It's Peters,
madam. He——' She choked, and her face crumpled,
then she turned and ran from the room, pushing the
butler aside in her haste to be gone.

'Well,' drawled Ryan, 'that's interesting.' He yawned
and ran his fingers through his hair.

'Come in, Peters.' Brittany pushed the bench back
from her dressing table and looked up at him. 'What was
that all about?'

The butler cleared his throat. 'It hurts me, madam, to have to come to you with this,' he said. 'If it was one of the housemaids, I'd have taken care of it myself. But since Felice is your personal maid——'

'Yes, Peters?'

'Felice was——' he coughed discreetly, and went on, 'She was discovered last night with a man in her room.'

'I'd told her she could have the rest of the evening off, Peters.'

'Horribly generous, that,' Ryan muttered. Brittany shot a quelling look at him.

Peters cleared his throat again. 'It wasn't simply a matter of her having a visitor, madam,' he said. 'He was in her bed, you see.'

'And that,' said Ryan, 'is no doubt the end of Felice.'

'What do you expect me to do?' Brittany shot back at him. 'I'm not running a boarding house here. Who knows where it would stop?' And she was the best maid I ever had, she thought.

'Quite so,' the butler agreed. 'I shall tell her that her services will no longer be required.'

Brittany sighed. 'No, I'll tell her myself,' she said.

Peters bowed. 'As you wish, madam.'

As soon as the door shut behind him, she turned on Ryan. 'Before you start your little lecture——' she began.

He shrugged. 'I was just wondering,' he said, 'who the man was.' Without another word, he retreated to the bathroom.

Brittany put her head in the door. 'What difference does it make?' she called through the hiss of water in the shower.

Ryan didn't answer. He had shed his pyjama jacket before he turned on the tap, and now he reached for the drawstring in the trousers. Brittany retreated without waiting for an answer.

Felice appeared in the doorway. Her white cap was

slightly askew, and her eyes were now not only puffy but red-rimmed in her blotchy face. 'You wanted to see me, madam?' she whispered.

'Felice,' Brittany began, shaking her head, 'you know I can't have this sort of thing in the servants' quarters. It's got nothing to do with your morals or mine, it's just that I can't allow my employees to indulge in this sort of conduct under my roof.'

'I know, madam,' Felice said miserably.

'I'm sorry, but——' Suddenly, Ryan's question popped to the tip of her tongue. 'Who was the man?' she found herself asking.

Felice sniffed. 'Ricky, madam. My husband.'

'Your—husband?' Brittany could hardly form the word. 'You've never said anything about being married!'

'Of course not, madam. The agency said you needed someone to live in, and to travel with you. A single girl, they said. Well, we needed the money, madam. Ricky hasn't got a steady job, and I thought—well, I thought it couldn't hurt you, what you didn't know.'

'Indeed!'

'But it was awful, being without Ricky.'

'I can imagine. And where does Ricky live?'

'He has an apartment with some friends. When I have my days off I go there, but we're never alone, and——'

'I see. So you brought Ricky here.'

Felice gulped and nodded. 'It's not the first time,' she confessed, low-voiced.

'You said that Ricky doesn't work?'

'Oh, no, madam! He works harder than anybody. But it's just that nobody needs him all the time, and even with his jobs and mine it's hard to get along. He can fix anything, my Ricky,' Felice said proudly. 'You should hear about some of his real neat ideas——' She caught herself, and stood up straight. 'I'm sorry for rattling on, madam,' she said primly.

'Ideas for things here at the Castle?'

Felice nodded, as if a little reluctant to admit that her husband had looked around the house.

'Well, we could use a handyman,' mused Brittany. 'I think you'd better bring Ricky to see me.'

Felice's eyes were round. 'Do you mean I'm not sacked?'

'If Ricky shows promise—well, there's an apartment over the carriage house that no one has used in some time. It's tiny, but it should be cosy enough for the two of you.'

Felice dropped to her knees. Tears were streaming down her face as she seized Brittany's hand and held it to her cheek. 'You're the best, most wonderful——'

Brittany was embarrassed. She looked up to see Ryan standing in the bathroom door, his hair still wet from the shower spray. How long had he been there? she wondered. And what would he say?

She only knew that she didn't want to hear it. 'Don't take any credit, Ryan,' she told him. Her voice was hard, defensive. 'Felice is the best maid I've ever had, and I'd be sorry to lose her. So you see, it's purely a selfish motive.'

'No one who knew you, Brittany,' he said, very softly, 'would ever suspect anything different.'

CHAPTER EIGHT

BRITTANY turned the pages of the morning newspaper, but even the headlines made no sense to her restless mind. She'd been waiting for Ryan for nearly an hour, and he had neither come home nor called. They were supposed to be arriving at the Curtises' lake cottage just about now. Instead, they would be running late and the whole weekend would get off to a bad start.

'And why it should be bothering me, I can't imagine,' Brittany muttered to herself. 'It's Ryan who wants that job, after all.'

She reached for the telephone. It had been so long since she'd called him at the legal clinic that she had to look up the number, and then as soon as the phone had started to ring, she regretted calling. She didn't want him to think she was checking up on him—after all, what did she care?

His secretary answered, prim and proper. Good old Mary Anderson, Brittany thought. Always loyal, always devoted to Ryan—ready to do anything necessary. Except for that one time, when her conscience had been able to stand no more, and then she had told Brittany the truth.

'He left just a few minutes ago,' Mary Anderson told her.

Brittany put the phone down, and wasted a moment wishing that she hadn't bothered. Could she trust what she was told, anyway? Even that time when Mary Anderson had confessed, Brittany had nearly had to batter the details from her.

She closed her eyes, shuddering, trying not to remember that awful day when Mary Anderson had told her about Diana Winslow, and about why Ryan had married Brittany. She had refused to believe it at first, had cried out that it wasn't true, none of it was true. 'Ryan loves me!' she had nearly screamed at the secretary. 'And losing the baby nearly killed him, too——'

The secretary had nodded sadly. 'Of course he's been upset about the miscarriage,' she said. Her voice was very quiet, but it seemed to Brittany to carry a ring of doom. 'A grandchild for your father would have cemented Mr Masters into the family. He's been on thin ice with Mr Bridges, over the legal clinic and all. The baby would have made it harder for Mr Bridges to refuse him what he wanted.'

'The vice-presidency at the bank,' Brittany had murmured.

Mary Anderson had nodded. There had been a gleam in her eyes just then, as if she was delighted that Brittany finally comprehended. 'That's what he's really wanted all along,' she explained. 'Authority at the bank.'

It had all made a horrible kind of sense to Brittany. Not even Mary Anderson knew that a few days before the miscarriage Brittany had overheard Clint and Ryan talking about First Federal. 'Brittany wants me to take a job at the bank,' Ryan had said. 'But corporate law—I don't know, Clint. It's never been what I wanted to do.'

Clint had grunted and answered, 'Well, let's all think it over, before we jump into anything. Maybe there'll be something else.'

She had wanted it; that was what had made it hardest to bear. She had pleaded with Ryan to give up his fledgling law practice. 'You can still be a lawyer,' she had told him. 'Daddy would be thrilled to have you at First Federal.' But all the time he had been pulling a kind of giant double bluff. Ryan had his heart set on bigger things. She had trusted Ryan, and he had betrayed that trust.

It was all long gone, and there was not much point in thinking about it now, she told herself. She got her heavy jacket and zipped it up as she stepped out of the back door. She'd walk around the grounds a little; Ryan would soon be home, and then she'd be shut up in a car with him for an hour's drive. She'd work off a little energy and frustration first.

It had been a week since the Foundation Christmas party. There had been no repetition of that forced kiss, with its unaccountable after-effects. She had made certain of that. She had simply stayed out of Ryan's way all week, and had swallowed her pride and started to sleep on the couch in their sitting room. Better safe and uncomfortable than to take a chance, she thought—though heaven knew, she was running little enough risk. That had been plain from the challenging sparkle in his eyes that first morning. Do this stupid thing if you want, he had seemed to be saying, but you're not proving anything.

She pulled the collar of her jacket up. Despite the cold, the windows were open in the tiny apartment above the carriage house. Brittany stood in the drive and looked up at it with a twinge of something that was almost envy.

When she had first unlocked the door of the apartment last weekend and shown Felice and Ricky in, Brittany had looked around the dirty, dark little rooms with a sense of loathing.

Felice had wrinkled her nose at the musty smell, pulled the ragged curtains back and opened a casement window. Then she had thrown her arms around Ricky. 'It's beautiful,' she smiled. 'We'll be happy here, won't we?'

Ricky had been a little slower to judge. He had walked through the rooms, then grinned down at Brittany. 'Nothing wrong here that a scrub brush and a little paint won't fix,' he had said. 'Thank you, ma'am.'

Brittany had looked around in shock. The dust was half an inch thick, the bits of furniture were mismatched and looked like rejects from a used-furniture store, the ceilings were low and sloping. It looked hopeless to her.

Since then, Felice had devoted every spare moment to the apartment. I wonder what it's like by now, Brittany thought, and climbed the steps.

Felice saw her coming and flung the door open. Her hair was tied back with a folded handkerchief, and there was a smudge of paint on her nose. She looked instantly concerned. 'Did you need me, madam?' she asked contritely.

'Heavens, no. I gave you the afternoon off—I just stopped by to see what the place looked like under all that dirt.'

Felice giggled. 'Awfully nice, if you ask me,' she said. 'Of course, Ricky's done most of the work so far—painting and building shelves.' She gestured towards the far wall. 'It's my turn next. I'm going to make new curtains and slipcover all the furniture, and then we'll have a cosy little nest.'

It looked cosy already to Brittany. And Felice had changed, too. Gone was the quiet, reserved little maid. Now Felice chattered and laughed, always respectful but seeming to bubble over with joy that she simply could not keep banked down. Her eyes were different, too. Now they seemed to have a glow.

Funny, Brittany thought, what a little thing like this had done for Felice—two tiny rooms, and the man she loved.

'Come in,' Felice begged. 'I've kept you standing out here in the cold——'

'No,' said Brittany. 'I just wanted to peep in.' Ryan's car pulled into the back drive, and she waved at him. 'Have a nice weekend,' she told Felice, and the girl grinned.

The first, alone in their new home—Brittany was certain it would be memorable. She stopped at the bottom of the steps and looked across the drive to the Castle. It was huge, high-ceilinged, room after room of space and gorgeous furniture. And yet somehow, she told herself, it had neither the light nor the warmth of those two tiny rooms . . .

Ryan had put her luggage in the car and was waiting impatiently. 'We're late already,' he said.

'And whose fault is that?' Brittany slid into the passenger seat.

'I see you've been visiting Felice,' he remarked, and backed the car out into the street.

'What business is it of yours?' Brittany asked irritably. 'I know that you've set yourself up as her protector, but——'

'It seems to me that there've been times when she needed protection.'

'Well, she has a husband for that now. You're out of a job.' She stared out of the window, tapping her fingers on the upholstery. 'Did you know she was married?' she asked at last.

'No. But I suspected it.'

'Why?'

'Because she didn't wear a ring—and yet there was an indentation on her finger, as if there should have been one there.' He glanced down at her hand on the seat. 'As there is on your finger right now. A place where there should be a ring, and isn't.'

Brittany inspected her left hand. Sure enough, at the base of the third finger was the evidence. 'I'm sorry if I upset you by giving my ring away,' she apologised. 'It was for a good cause, you know.'

'It doesn't bother me in the least,' he said. 'As long as you don't start pretending that it was any great sacrifice. We both know you did it to get even with me, and not because the Foundation needed the money.'

Brittany shrugged. 'Whatever the reason, it's gone now.' She sighed. 'It was a shame, actually. That was a beautiful star sapphire.'

'Don't expect me to fall for that line. Gifts that really have meaning hurt the giver just a little, Brittany. It isn't

true generosity if you give away only the excess. Your
ring was excess property—and like Alex Warren's
diamond bracelet, only the accountants will benefit in
the end.'

Brittany looked at him with unconcealed dislike and
said tartly, 'Well, I'm glad you didn't forget to polish your
halo this morning!'

'I believe I've asked you before to wear a wedding ring.
And you do still own one.'

She shrugged. 'Sorry. I keep forgetting to pick it up.'

Ryan fumbled in his pocket. 'Luckily I didn't.' He
thrust the engraved band at her.

Brittany studied it. She hadn't worn this ring since
their wedding day, when she had tugged it off her finger
immediately after the ceremony and demanded that he
give her the sapphire one.

There was no sense in fighting him about it, she
decided, and slid the ring on to her finger. It was warm
from his body heat. If it hadn't been for that, she
wouldn't have felt it at all.

She turned to the window and spent the rest of the
drive staring out at the snow. Shopping areas gave way to
suburbs and then to small towns, country roads and
fields. What a dreary day! she thought. The grey sky was
low and threatening, as if pressing down to smother the
world. And what a dreary weekend lay ahead, with only
the Curtises for companionship.

Mrs Curtis greeted them, unconcerned by their
lateness, with hot apple cider and crisp cookies. 'It's one
of the things I like best about the cottage,' she confided to
Brittany. 'At the Mansion, I'm too busy to spend much
time in the kitchen, and when I get there, there are
always a couple of people underfoot, and I do so love to
bake!' She urged another ginger snap on Ryan. 'There
are disadvantages to big houses,' she added wisely.

Brittany nodded politely, and thought she was unable
to think of a single disadvantage. Then that tiny twinge

of jealousy she had felt towards Felice crept back into her mind. She shook it away and told herself that it had nothing to do with houses.

'Dan went into town to pick up a few more supplies,' Mrs Curtis finished. 'He'll be back in a little while, and we're going to grill steaks tonight. But we want you to feel right at home. And we know how precious your weekends are, and how much you've given up to spend this one with us. So if you want to be alone, you just go right ahead. We won't be hurt at all.' She smiled. 'In fact, why don't you start now? It's still light enough for a walk down by the lake. Run along, and have a good time.'

'I'll bet that's the way she talked to her kids when they were toddlers,' grumbled Brittany as they crossed the frozen grass to the snow-covered sand. 'Have you ever seen anything so bleak?' She pointed out across the wind-whipped waves.

Ryan seemed not to have heard.

Brittany thought about repeating herself, then thought, what's the use? He doesn't want to talk to me, he doesn't want to have anything to do with me——

Tears burned at the back of her eyes, then anger started to build in the pit of her stomach. She stooped, scooped up a handful of snow, and flung it full in his face.

He jumped, swore, wiped the snow from his eyes, and demanded, 'What the devil was that all about?' Then the grim set of his jaw relaxed. 'So you want to have a snowball fight, do you?' he asked, and retaliated in one smooth motion so fast that his arm was almost a blur.

Brittany ducked behind a tree, but the snowball caught her in the shoulder. She tried to fight back, but her aim was no match for Ryan's. In a matter of minutes she had been pelted, and snow was melting down her collar, sinking into her low boots, and crusting on her knitted cap. 'Pax!' she cried finally, breathlessly. 'I give up!'

Ryan peered around a tree. 'You never could aim worth a darn,' he said, and she hit him square on the nose with a loose snowball. It exploded over his face, and she doubled over with laughter as he spluttered through the mask.

He came after her then, and ran her down in the woods before she could reach the safety of the house. 'You'll pay,' he warned.

Brittany tripped over a protruding root. She tried to twist in order to break her fall, but she went down heavily, knocking her breath out. For a dreadful space of moments, she could barely breathe.

Ryan knelt beside her. 'You'll be fine,' he said. 'Don't try so hard.'

'Why?' she wheezed. 'You want me—to die—out here?' But in a minute, the pain eased, and she started to sit up.

Ryan pushed her back down into the snow. 'How long has it been since you made a snow angel?' he demanded.

'But I'll get all wet!'

'That's half the fun.' He held her down in the snow, ignoring her protests, and dragged her arms up and down till the angel's wings were outlined to his satisfaction. Snow oozed under her coat and tingled against her bare back where her jeans and sweater had parted company. 'People who don't play fair deserve any kind of treatment the opposition hands out,' he teased.

'I'll play fair,' she gasped. 'Just let me get up——'

He was crouching over her in the snow. Her cap had come off, and her hair was spread over the ground, tangled against the white crystals. Her breath was coming fast, in anxious little pants, and she was helpless with his hands locked on her wrists.

It was the first time she had been so close to him in a week. She looked up into his eyes, and saw that the laughter had died out of them. His grip on her wrists relaxed, and he lowered himself down to the ground beside her.

'No!' she breathed, but the faint protest was lost in the heat of his lips against hers, and suddenly she wasn't cold any more.

His kiss was gentle, but the effect on Brittany was devastating none-the-less. Her breath was coming in constricted little gasps, and her traitorous body seemed to want to mould itself to his, to pull him down closer and closer until they were one.

Ryan released her mouth, only to feather kisses across her cheek, her temple, her throat.

Why? she thought. Why does he have this power over me? It isn't fair—he's hurt me so badly, and yet he can make me feel like this!

They lay there silent in the snow for a moment, then a rustle in the branches above them came as a warning. 'Sleet,' said Ryan. He rolled to his feet and reached a hand down to Brittany. 'The storm finally got here. We'll have to run for it.'

By the time they reached the house, raindrops were falling all around them, freezing in the air and as soon as they hit the ground. The redwood veranda at the back of the cabin was already wet.

Governor Curtis was standing at the plate glass window, looking out on to the woods, when they came in. He gestured with the mug he held. 'I thought we might have to send a search party out for you,' he said cheerfully. 'Have you been building a snowman?'

'Nothing quite that constructive,' Ryan said.

'Well, you'd better get out of those wet clothes,' Dan insisted. 'We'll keep the chocolate hot for you. I'll show you to your room.'

The guest quarters were comfortable, but not large. There was a big bed, a pair of comfortable chairs, a dressing table. There was no way to escape it here; they would have to share a bed.

Brittany looked the room over, and sighed. I won't make a fuss about it, she told herself firmly. If I did, Ryan would only laugh at me. After all, we slept together for two weeks at the Castle. This will be no different.

She opened her bag and pulled out a dressing gown. 'I'll hurry in the shower,' she said.

He was staring out of the window. 'Do you know,' he said thoughtfully, 'I haven't done anything like that in years.'

'Neither have I,' said Brittany. 'Perhaps tomorrow we should build a snow fort.' At least, she thought, it would keep them occupied, and prevent any of that competition which seemed to have sparked the trouble today.

Ryan shook his head. 'I'll bet there'll be an inch of ice by morning,' he said. 'Look at that sleet coming down! Besides,' he turned to look her over, 'your idea of building a snow fort is probably to hire an architect and a contractor.'

Brittany wanted to throw something at him. Instead, she retreated silently to the tiny bathroom.

And it's only Friday evening, she told herself miserably. *I have to get through a whole weekend of this.*

She went to sleep with icy determination to stay on the very edge of the bed. And she woke snuggled into a ball in the exact centre of it, with Ryan's body curved protectively around her own, afraid to move for fear she would wake him. The travel clock on the bedside table said it was five in the morning.

Well, at least that was nothing unusual, she told herself. She'd been waking at fearsomely early hours, on that uncomfortable couch. This was really no different. All she had to do was edge carefully away from Ryan and go back to sleep on her own side of the bed. She stretched a toe out; the blankets were uncomfortably chilly against her bare skin.

'There's nothing to get up for,' he said sleepily. 'The power went off about midnight. Go back to sleep.' He hadn't even opened his eyes, and in another minute a tiny snore told her just how excited he had been about finding her in his arms.

She put a hand out tentatively, and drew it back in shock; the air in the bedroom felt frigid. He hadn't been dreaming about the electricity going off!

She tried to settle down again. But she was thoroughly awake now, and shudderingly aware of the warmth of his body against her, and the hard strength of his arms around her. His forearm lay snuggled beneath her breasts; with every breath he took, his chest pressed against her back.

Brittany lay there quietly in his arms, trying not to breathe at all, and fought against the memories of the way it used to be, in the days when she had been certain of his love.

It had been a beautiful few months. They had been as innocently joyful as Felice and Ricky were, exploring the world of love and probing the depths of their passion. If someone had asked her then whether their marriage was a success, Brittany would have laughed at the question. Of course it was, she would have said; of course it was.

So, what had happened to them?

It wasn't Ryan, she thought. And it hadn't even been Diana; that had come later. Looking back now, she knew there had been trouble between them before Diana came along. It was Brittany herself who had changed.

Hot tears burned her eyes. So what if he had married her for her father's money? Marriages had been based on less, and had been successful. Most marriages were a trade-off of some sort; both husband and wife gained benefits from the partnership. An alliance for financial gain was certainly nothing new. So what if Ryan had wanted the money? She had wanted Ryan.

Why was I so idealistic, she wondered, so rigid? I should have been happy to have him at all. And he did care about me, then. Perhaps it wasn't the kind of adoration I wanted from a husband, but then perhaps I didn't give him what he needed, either.

Respect, for one thing, she thought painfully.

A great many of their problems had been her fault. He had turned to Diana Winslow, that was true. But had Brittany not driven him to it?

As soon as she had suspected her pregnancy, she had practically put Ryan out of her life altogether. And even before that, there had been trouble.

She had changed after their wedding, she thought painfully, remembering little things that had seemed so unimportant at the time. She had no longer taken time to be with him, to do the silly little things of their courtship. Because there were things about her world that he didn't know, and didn't care about, she had begun to think he was stupid. Because he had not been like her friends, she had lost her respect for him—and yet that difference had been the very reason she had married him!

The tears spilled over, burning streaks down the side of her face. No wonder he had turned to Diana, she thought humbly. For Diana had never made it any secret that she thought Ryan was brilliant.

I had my chance, Brittany told herself, and I wasted it. Or had she? Was it entirely gone?

He married me, she reminded herself firmly. Whatever the reason, it doesn't change the fact. And he is still my husband. I can fight for him——

'Tears?' Ryan's voice was still gruff with sleep as he raised himself on one elbow and looked down at her. 'It isn't the end of the world, you know. Despite the ice, we won't freeze or starve, and we won't be stuck here for the winter.' His mouth brushed her temple, kissing the tears away.

Brittany tensed for an instant, then she turned her back on the past. 'Ryan,' she whispered, 'I'm so lonely.'

He was still for an instant, assessing what she had said. 'What's the price, Brittany?' he said, but he didn't sound angry, only sad.

Recklessly, she twisted around in his arms. Her fingers wandered across his chest, up his neck, through his hair. 'No price,' she said, and felt like a brazen hussy. 'Please. I don't want to be alone any more.'

His eyes were dark, incredulous. For an instant she was afraid that he would reject her, that he would fling some cynical comment at her. He seemed to struggle with himself, fighting some private war. Then his arms tightened very slowly around her, drawing her closer and ever closer to the warmth of his body.

Now that it was too late to change her mind, she almost panicked. What have I done? she thought.

But as he kissed her, she knew that however much she might regret this action later, at the moment she would not have changed an instant.

Ryan was gentle as he re-explored her body, bending his head to caress her breast, stroking her silken skin with the very tips of his fingers. It was a simple, sensual trick he had learned long ago, she remembered, one that had always reduced her to a quivering, mindless thing. Its magic worked once more, and left her no more in control of her body than if it had been constructed of rubber bands.

Did he make love to Diana like this? she wondered, and banished the traitorous thought from her mind. It didn't matter, she told herself. She was his wife, not Diana. She still had a few weapons at her command.

And so she sighed deep in her throat, and pulled him down to her, and told him with every sinew of her body that she was sorry for the years that had gone by. Those wasted years, she thought, that might have brought them some happiness through this shared tenderness. For even if they had nothing else together they had this...

Their lovemaking had an almost frantic quality to it, she thought, as if they both knew they were hiding from the world, and that some day they would have to face the future.

And then, as they reached together for the ultimate glory, she could no longer think at all, only feel, and know that for all time, this was where she wanted to be—in the arms of the only man who could ever make her feel like this.

CHAPTER NINE

THE electricity stayed off all weekend. The weight of the sleet and freezing rain had been too much for the wires to bear, and though the crews worked around the clock, the isolated cottage was near the end of the lines.

The State police brought in an emergency generator, which Dan Curtis waved away. 'You brought that thing here just because I'm the Governor?' he had demanded. 'Take it to the next cabin down the road—those people have children they're trying to keep warm.'

He closed the door behind the trooper, put another log on the fireplace, and said to Brittany, 'I hope you don't mind. We can manage, but those youngsters——'

Brittany shook her head, thinking dreamily that the only thing she minded was the interruptions. If it wasn't for the State police constantly skating in with a message for the Governor, they might have been here alone, like pioneers on a prairie . . . She didn't even mind having the company of the Curtises, she realised; they were nothing more than a pair of indulgent chaperones.

The Governor lit his pipe with an ember from the fire, sucked on it till it was drawing just right, rubbed his hands together and said, 'Now, let's get back to the real business of the world. How about a little more cut-throat poker? Britt, will you back me with a loan? Ryan cleaned me out of fifty-two cents last round.'

'How's your credit rating?' she asked, and watched the poker game settle down to some serious bluffing.

She had slept late that morning, relaxed and satiated, and rose feeling lazy, to find Ryan and Dan Curtis already feeding a snapping fire in the living room.

Ryan had been quiet, as if reluctant to talk at all. It hadn't surprised Brittany, who looked at it as a sort of reprieve. What had happened the night before had been beyond her comprehension; she didn't want to try to explain it.

She tried her hand at cooking breakfast on the old cast-iron wood-burning stove, and admitted that there was more of a knack to it than she had thought. They read and played and dreamed the daylight away, and still they didn't talk, Brittany thought. At least not to each other; even if they had wanted to, there was no time.

Even when they were alone together that night in the cool bedroom in the winter darkness, they had little to say to each other. The sensual memory of the night before haunted Brittany, making it impossible to sleep. Ryan had turned his back to her and lay rigidly still; that didn't make it any easier for her to bear. Did he regret so deeply what had happened the night before? She tossed restlessly, and more than once brushed against Ryan's body.

Finally he turned, and his arm was like a bar across her body, pressing her back against the pillows. 'Would you lie still?' he hissed. 'I can't stand this——'

She hadn't done it on purpose, but she had moved, and her breasts had pressed against his arm. That tiny movement had triggered a storm that raged between them. There was no gentleness this time, no careful caresses, no tender kisses. Instead, this coupling was the fierceness of two bodies clamouring for physical satiation, without concern at the moment for anything else. And it was satisfying in a way that no gentler lovemaking had ever been.

And so the weekend went. The daylight hours were sane and quiet. They laughed at the Governor's jokes, and gave a willing hand to help with the work, with only a look exchanged now and then that hinted of the simmering emotions that lurked beneath the smooth surface, and burst forth in increasing passion when darkness fell and found them alone together.

Both of them, Brittany thought, knew that it was an ill-fated attempt to hide from the past, to pretend that none of those awful things had mattered. She was torn between reason and desire, knowing that she should preserve good sense and dignity by turning away from Ryan. And yet, when she tried, she found herself in his arms anyway, begging, pleading, demanding satisfaction for her body, while her mind screamed that this was foolish, stupid, criminal . . .

Ryan, she thought, felt much the same way. He, too, seemed to be fighting a battle within himself. Each time they were alone, he ultimately surrendered, and reached out to her with a groan that expressed a fierce hunger, touching something primitive in her as well. Each time, the hunger seemed to grow, and the reluctance as well.

She had caught him once looking at her with an expression that was almost a scowl, as if he was trying to puzzle out a problem. She knew then, with a shame that cut to her very soul, that if Ryan merely looked at her, she was suddenly aflame with longing.

He can make me feel more possessed with a look, she thought, than any other man ever could. The idea humbled her, it tormented her, it horrified her. It solidified her determination to stop this madness. But that night, in his arms, she forgot everything except that she was with him.

The weekend was a moment frozen in time, and she told herself over and over that she would be glad when it was done. And yet, when the power hummed through the lines again on Sunday evening, and the electric lights came to life, Brittany found herself feeling very sad, knowing that it could never again be quite the same.

They drove back to the city over patchy ice early on Monday morning, and went to work. The silence of the weekend had continued in the car. There simply seemed to be nothing to say. It wasn't an uncomfortable silence, precisely, Brittany thought, and yet it wasn't an easy one, either. It was as if they were afraid of words.

The executive floors at First Federal were almost deserted that morning. Downstairs, the tellers were busy, almost flooded by the last-minute deposits and withdrawals as the Christmas shopping season entered its final frantic day. The bank would close early because it was Christmas Eve, and everyone, it seemed, was pushing a whole week's business into the morning hours. But upstairs, the pace was quiet, and many of the executives had taken this extra day off to celebrate the holiday.

Brittany tried to work, but she quickly discovered that most of the people she needed to talk to had gone home for the holiday. The ones she did reach didn't want to make decisions until after Christmas.

'I'm just marking time,' she told herself. 'I might as well give up.' She poured herself a cup of coffee and wandered down the hall towards Clint's office. She still needed to talk to him; at least that was something she could do.

They were all just marking time, waiting, she thought. She and Ryan were waiting for the Governor's decision, waiting for the announcement, waiting for the job.

That was why they had been silent, she realised; there was nothing to talk about. Until Dan Curtis chose his consumer advocate, they could not plan. If Ryan got the job, she found herself thinking, then they would have to keep up the front for a while. He had said himself that the divorce would have to be put off for a little while, until he was established. And if he didn't get the job . . .

Brittany found herself shivering. He has to get it, she

thought, and told herself that she was so concerned only because she feared what he might do next. The important thing now was to get Ryan that position; she wouldn't let herself think any further than that. Ryan had said once that Clint's influence might make the difference. Very well, she decided, she would ask Clint to lend his weight to the cause.

She knocked on his door and went in.

Clint looked up from his putter and then ignored her for the next full minute. The putt missed, and he sighed and put the club aside.

'Hopeless,' he said. 'I'm getting worse instead of better. These mechanical aids are worse than useless, and even if the putting practice helped, I'd hate to see what I'm like these days on a driving range.'

'Nothing substitutes for the real thing,' Brittany agreed.

'Are you certain you won't go to Palm Springs with me? Ryan wouldn't mind. He might even take a break himself and come along.'

'That's what I came to talk to you about.'

His eyes brightened. 'Palm Springs?'

'No. Ryan.'

'Oh.' Clint picked up his putter again. He sounded absorbed as he asked, 'What now?'

'He really wants that job, Dad. We spent the weekend trying to charm the Governor, but he's a sly old fox. Do you suppose you could convince him?'

'So now you're lobbying the old man, Britt?'

'If you'd just use your influence with Dan Curtis——,' she began. Clint merely looked at her in surprise. 'If you want me to,' he said. 'No promises, though,' he added firmly. 'I refuse to put my friendship with Dan Curtis on the line over a job for Ryan.'

'Fair enough.'

Clint took a practice swing, and shook his head. 'I

didn't think Ryan was serious for a moment about that job. Leave law, to go into public service?'

'That's what he wants, Dad.'

He looked up, his eyes suddenly piercing. 'And what do you want, Britt? You used to be set on the idea of him working for the bank.'

For a moment her heart froze. If Clint were to offer a vice-presidency now, Ryan would jump at it, she was sure. But that would mean that he would have to stay at the Castle——

Was that what she wanted? she asked herself, almost in terror. Did she want Ryan to stay? Was that what her uncontrolled longings had been trying to tell her all weekend?

But could she ask Clint to make a job for Ryan? Did she want him at all, if that was the way it had to be? she asked herself.

She lost herself for a moment in a vision of what life could be if Ryan stayed at the Castle. The joy that sprang to life in her heart shocked her, and ruthless honesty forced her to admit the truth: she wanted him, no matter what it took to keep him there.

But an older and wiser Brittany knew that it had to be his decision. She would no longer go behind his back to arrange his life. 'Perhaps you'd better talk to him about that, Dad,' she said softly.

Her father didn't comment, but his bright eyes seemed to look through her very soul. Then he bent down to place another practice ball on the carpet.

'Lydia's going to Florida next month,' she said, almost as an afterthought. 'And she plays golf.'

'I know.'

Brittany leaned forward, propped her elbows on the desk, laced her fingers together and rested her chin on them. 'Why don't you join her?'

'Hell,' he muttered, and took a vicious swing at the

plastic ball. 'She doesn't want to be bothered with an old duffer like me,' he said finally. 'If Lydia had any use for men, she'd have been married long ago. She only puts up with me because of her friendship with your mother.'

'In the first place,' Brittany said quietly, 'you're not old, and Lydia isn't a great deal younger.' She started for the door.

'That sounds as if there's more to come,' said Clint. He was leaning on his putter.

Brittany turned at the door. 'I've often wondered,' she said, 'if Lydia didn't stay single because the one man she wanted was already married.'

'And just what does that mean?'

Brittany shrugged. 'It's only speculation,' she said, and hoped Lydia would forgive the white lie. 'I think I'll go on home now. Don't be late today, Dad.'

'Wouldn't miss Christmas Eve at the Castle for the world,' he assured her, 'now that we're a family again.'

There was a twinge in the pit of her stomach. She didn't like to lie to her father.

But maybe it isn't a lie, she told herself stoutly. If Ryan gets that job . . . No, I won't even admit that there's any doubt. *When* Ryan gets that job . . . Or if Dad gives him a position at the bank . . .

Sara Whittaker was just coming out of Brittany's office. 'I thought I'd missed you,' she said.

'I'm sorry you aren't coming to spend Christmas with us,' said Brittany.

'So am I, but I think it's important that Amanda and I start building traditions for the two of us.'

'Well, I can't quarrel with that, but we'll miss you.'

Sara smiled. 'You look different these days,' she observed. 'As though you've slowed down a little, and been sleeping well for a change.'

Brittany felt a blush creep up her face.

Sara didn't push the issue. 'What I really came up to

talk to you about was the problem Eric Rhodes is having with that accounts clerk.'

'The crazy lady? Come on in and tell me what you found.'

'She's not crazy,' said Sara quietly.

'Sorry—it was careless of me to use the term. What's wrong with her?'

'That's just it, Brittany. Nothing is wrong with her. Nothing at all.'

There was a silent moment while Brittany tried to absorb the information. 'Have you told Eric that?'

'Of course I have. Mr Rhodes doesn't want to talk about it. He's written her off as a split personality now—though where he got his psychiatric training is beyond me!' Sara sounded half amused, half angry.

'You seem very upset.'

'I am. He's already suspended her, and he's started the proceedings to fire her, and there's no reason for it. She's probably the best worker in the department.'

Brittany frowned. Could this doctor, good as she was, have missed something?

Sara saw the doubt in Brittany's eyes. 'Look, I'll show you the test results if you like. The woman passed every standard diagnostic test. She's normal.'

'Are you qualified to give those tests?'

'To give them, yes. To interpret them, no—therefore in next month's clinic bills you'll find a payment to the psychologist who did. He's the head of the department at the university.'

'I see.'

Sara sighed. 'She gave me a folder of things for you— questionable invoices that she'd slipped out of the files before Mr Rhodes suspended her, comparisons of past years, that sort of thing. She's even drawn charts.'

'She shouldn't have those invoices,' protested Brittany.

'Don't be so rigid! Before you condemn her, look the folder over and see if you can make any sense of it. I certainly can't—but she's on to something.'

'All right,' Brittany said reluctantly.

'Good.' Sara sighed. 'I don't know what's going on in Accounts Payable, but if there's anything mentally wrong with that woman, I'll eat my medical diploma in the lobby at high noon!'

A bit chastened, Brittany went back to her desk. A fat file folder lay on the blotter. She started to thumb through it, and then dropped it into her briefcase. It was Christmas, after all. The problem in Accounts Payable could wait till after the holiday.

Christmas Day was winding to a close. It had ended up with just the four of them, Clint and Lydia, Ryan and Brittany. Brittany's plans for a party had fallen through, but she didn't regret it. As it was, it had been a quiet, comfortable day.

Funny, she thought, how just a week ago she had been dreading this day with Ryan. And now that it was nearly gone, she wished it would never end. Except for one thing, she thought, with colour rising in her cheeks; she knew that tonight, in their big bed upstairs, they would once again find the closeness that eluded them everywhere else. She should be ashamed of herself, she thought, for being impatient to be in his arms again.

He was absorbed in the football game. She sat beside him for a while, but she couldn't concentrate on the game, and she lacked patience to work on her needlepoint. Restlessness tugged at her, the vague feeling that there was something important she should be doing.

She wandered through the house, enjoying the silence. After the big Christmas dinner had been served, the staff members had scattered to their own holidays, and the Castle was quiet. Clint and Lydia had gone for a walk;

Brittany thought she had seen a new determination in her father's eyes, and hoped her bit of meddling would have good results.

She paused beside a closed door, then, biting her lip, went into the room that would have been the nursery. She realised, with slight surprise, that this was the first time all day that she had even thought about the baby she had lost.

She looked around the big, airy room. It was just another guest room now, of course; the plans had been made, but she had only started to accumulate the nursery furniture when she had the miscarriage.

She sat down on the foot of a twin bed. Just about here, she thought, was where she would have put a rocking chair. And there was where her own crib would have stood, draped in a lacy canopy. There was nostalgia in her thoughts, but the stabbing pain that had been such a part of her whenever she thought of the baby had died to a tiny ache in a corner of her heart.

On Christmases past, the memory of the child had haunted her. It was worse, she knew, because the baby would have been born in the middle of the Christmas season.

Ryan had said, when she had first told him about the pregnancy, that a baby was the best gift a man could ever receive. Instead, that first Christmas had been a lonely torture for Brittany, without the baby and with only the bittersweet memories of her husband to wrap around her in the cold nights.

And had that first Christmas also been lonely torture for Ryan? Funny, she thought, that she had never wondered about that before. Had he mourned their loss, as she had? Or had Mary Anderson been right in saying that he cared about the baby only in order to cement his own position with Clint? Had it even been a sort of relief for him, to have the thread between them broken?

In any case, what does it matter now? Brittany asked herself. It was far too late. Too much time had passed, too many bitter things had been said, too many hurtful actions had been taken. It was too late to mend their broken marriage.

He must once have cared a little, she thought sadly. Now even that was gone, destroyed by her selfishness and spoiled arrogance. Now all that was left was the passion they shared.

She didn't even know she was crying, then. She cried for herself, of course, but also for the dreams of youth, and for the lost idealism that had made them believe that love could conquer the differences between them, and make them one.

The truth is, she told herself, I didn't know what love was, then. I didn't know it hurt to love someone.

And did she still love him?

It was a quiet question, and the answer that echoed through her mind came as no shock. Of course she loved Ryan. Brittany knew now, deep within herself, that she had always loved him. If she had been less spoiled, less selfish, she would have fought for him two years ago. The baby had been their only chance, he had said. But there could have been another baby, if she hadn't let her wounded pride drive her into sending him away.

She had been so proud, and so hurt by what she had seen as his treachery, that she had told herself she didn't want him at all, and she had discarded Ryan, and their marriage, with a careless wave of the hand.

Except it refused to stay discarded. In the two years since, she had met no man who could touch her as Ryan could, either physically or emotionally.

She bowed her head, and admitted to herself what her heart had known for years—that there was no man for her except Ryan, and that she wanted him, needed him, loved him above anything else on earth.

She sat there for a long time, mourning for the foolish girl she had been. But then a fragment of hope probed into the back of her mind. Wasn't it possible, she thought, that Ryan had also suffered from their separation? After all, she reminded herself, he had not asked for a divorce. He had worn his wedding ring through the long years——

I'll go downstairs to him, she told herself, and wiped tears off her cheeks with a hasty hand. I'll throw myself down at his feet and tell him that I need him, that I love him, that I'll do whatever he wants me to do, and be whatever he wants me to be. And then perhaps, some day, he might come to care about me again—maybe even to love me.

She could think no further than that. She splashed cold water on her face and hurried down the steps.

Her father and Lydia were in the front hall. 'There you are,' said Clint. 'Ryan told us you'd come upstairs. We were looking for you.'

There was a note in his voice that startled her, and for an instant she forgot what she had been in such a hurry to do. Lydia's face was pleasantly pink from her walk—or was it only the exercise? Brittany asked herself. Then she saw the soft glow in Lydia's eyes, and she knew.

'Talk about telltale faces!' she laughed, and put her arms around Lydia.

'You did tell me,' Clint said, a little self-consciously, 'that you wouldn't mind having a stepmother.'

'Mind?' Brittany echoed. 'I'm astounded at your good taste, Dad.'

Lydia laughed, just a little nervously. 'Thank you, Brittany,' she whispered.

'When is the wedding?'

'As soon as possible,' said Clint.

Brittany said, 'In that case, I have to tell you that I'm shocked.'

Clint raised an eyebrow. 'Why?' he asked. 'Because I'm the man Lydia was waiting for?'

'No. I think she's a wise woman. It's this unseemly haste. Do you know what your acquaintances are going to say?'

'That I'm a smart man,' Clint muttered.

'And as for me,' Brittany went on, 'I was prepared for an old-fashioned courtship—walks in the moonlight, and kisses on the hand. But this hurry—why, it's positively indecent!'

'And you,' her father growled, 'can cut it out any time. At my age, I haven't time for walks in the moonlight.'

'None?' Brittany asked sadly. 'What a waste!'

'So we'll take walks after the wedding. In Florida.'

'Oh, I see. Watch out, Lydia—you'll be spending the rest of your life on a golf course somewhere.'

'Not all of it,' said Clint. 'Let's go over to your house, Lydia.'

'Without a chaperone?' Brittany did her best to sound horrified.

He eyed her warily. 'Let's leave the little lady here to chortle—we don't have to listen to this.'

Brittany sobered and put an arm around each of them. 'I'm sorry,' she said. 'I think it's lovely that you've found each other, and if you'd like to be married here at the Castle, I'd be delighted to throw the biggest reception you've ever seen.'

Lydia kissed her gently. 'We'll see,' she said. 'We haven't talked about the details yet.'

Clint put his arm around her. 'Britt,' he said, with a break in his voice, 'thank you. If it hadn't been for you, I'd have never got up the nerve to ask her!'

Brittany hugged them both, saw them off, shut the door behind them, and heaved a happy sigh. Then, with a new determination added, she turned towards her sitting room.

The television had been turned off, and Ryan was sitting there staring at the blank screen.

'Did Dad and Lydia tell you their news?' Brittany asked brightly. She curled up in a chair.

'Yes.' He didn't seem to care.

'I told them we'd have a reception for them here. It should be fun.'

'Yes.' He looked up, at last, with a sigh. 'Leave me out of it, Brittany.'

'What? Surely you don't object! They are consenting adults, after all, and——'

'It has nothing to do with Clint and Lydia.' He stood up. 'I just meant that whenever the wedding is, I won't be here. I'm sure Eric would love to play host.'

She was stunned, so startled that he had left the room before she found her voice. 'Ryan!' she called, following him up the stairs.

By the time she had reached their suite, he had pulled a closet door open and was piling clothes at random in a suitcase.

That alone would have told her how upset he was, she thought. Ryan never tossed clothes around, or left them lying about. He had always cared for his things, as if he knew quite clearly that if he mistreated one item there would never be another to take its place.

'Why?' she whispered. Her voice was hoarse. She felt as if the room was spinning around her. There had been no hint of this. What could have happened? They had barely exchanged a word all day; surely she had done nothing to provoke this——

'Where are you going?' she asked. 'You gave up your apartment——'

'God knows I've spent the night on the sofa in my office before.'

'What happened?' she demanded. You can't leave now, she thought. You must give me a chance!

For a moment, she thought he hadn't heard. Then he said, without so much as turning his head, 'I was only here because of one thing, Brittany—waiting until the Governor made his announcement. Well, he made it today. It was on the news, right after the football game.'

'But——' They couldn't split up now, she thought, in panic. They had to wait till he was settled in the job, and secure——

'And it wasn't me that he chose,' Ryan said flatly. He closed the case and snapped the locks. The metallic click was eerily loud in the quiet room.

'So I'm getting out of this prison,' he added, 'while I still have my sanity left.'

Brittany sat down heavily, on the end of the *chaise-longue*. She couldn't speak. She stretched out a pleading hand towards him, but he ignored it.

His footsteps echoed down the marble steps, and the front door banged as he slammed it. The sound seemed to reverberate through her body.

He's gone, she thought. And now there's nothing left at all.

CHAPTER TEN

CLINT found her curled into a miserable ball on the couch in her downstairs sitting room. She had wept herself into exhaustion, then sat there motionless, a handkerchief crumpled into a hard ball in her hand, her cheek against a cushion that was soaked with her tears. She had no idea how long she had been sitting there, and she no longer cared. She didn't even move when he came in.

'Brittany!' He sounded horrified. He crossed the room to her with quick strides, snapped on a light to banish the dimness, and dropped to one knee beside her. 'What's the matter?'

'Daddy.' It was the exhausted whimper of a child, and she buried her face in his shoulder. She was too tired to cry any more. 'Ryan's gone . . .'

She confessed the whole sorry story, from the beginning, how she and Ryan had planned and schemed and lied to convince the Governor. Her voice was quiet, flat, unemotional.

Clint held her close and whispered soothing nothings into her ear until her story was finished. Then, with a sigh, he said, 'Oh, Brittany sweetheart——' There was sadness in his voice, but not even a hint of anger or surprise.

The understanding tone brought fresh tears. Where the flood came from Brittany would never know, for she thought she had cried herself out long since. She would not have been surprised if her father had scolded her for this stupid trick; that he felt only sympathy was the astonishing thing.

Clint stroked her hair till her sobs passed and her

rasping breathing eased. 'And he heard the announcement on the news, you said?'

She nodded wearily.

He looked furious, his jaw clenched. His hand was
folding and unfolding as if he'd like to slam his fist into
something, but hadn't quite decided what.

I'm glad he isn't mad at me, she thought, then asked
herself, what if he goes after Ryan?

'You aren't going to hurt Ryan, are you?' she asked,
with a catch in her voice.

Clint smiled grimly. 'Do you want me to?'

'No—please, no, Dad.'

He sobered, then. 'Of course I'm not going to go after
Ryan,' he said. 'It seems to me there's been plenty of
hurting going on as it is.' His eyebrows were drawn
together in a frown. Then, as if his decision was made, he
reached for the telephone.

'Who are you calling?' She was instantly panicky. 'Not
Ryan——'

'No,' he said. 'I think Ryan needs a chance to cool off.'
His call was answered, and he said, 'This is Clint
Bridges. I need to talk to Governor Curtis.' Then, a
moment later, 'Yes, dammit, it is important. It's
Christmas over here, too, you know. If it wasn't
important I wouldn't be calling.'

'Please, Dad.' Brittany sniffed once. It was some
comfort to know that he was ready to do this. As always,
her father was there to do whatever he could to ease his
little girl's hurt. But this time there was nothing anyone
could do. The Bridges money can't buy everything, she
thought. Sometimes it can't buy much at all.

'Don't do this to me,' she pleaded. 'Don't beg. You
can't buy Ryan back, with that job or any other!'

'I'm not buying anything,' he said impatiently. 'And
I'm not begging, either.' He turned away from her. 'Dan?
I hear you have a new consumer advocate. What the hell

happened?'

Brittany huddled on the couch and twisted her wedding ring as she tried not to listen. It hurt unbearably to have them discussing her like this; it tore her to shreds when she even thought about it. All the innocent plans she had made, the easy determination to do anything necessary to make Ryan happy, to keep him with her—how stupid she had been! He wanted nothing to do with her. If it had not been for that job, he would never have willingly spoken to her again. The dream she had cherished that he might agree to stay with her, and that he might some day love her, was too painful to think about now.

She had even been lying to herself about the passion she had thought they shared. He was a man, after all, she told herself stoically, with a willing woman in his arms. Of course he had made love to her. It would have made no difference to him which woman was there with him.

'Dammit, Dan, you promised!' Clint said finally. There was another long explanation from the other end of the line, and then Clint sighed. 'All right, I understand. I'll tell her.'

He put the telephone down and turned back to Brittany. 'Honey,' he said heavily, 'it was a mistake.'

Her heart seemed to jump into her throat, and then she hated herself even more for falling into that trap again. Ryan had made it perfectly clear, what he thought of her. It could make no difference, now, whoever ended up with that job. She still had her pride, after all . . .

But her throat was raw with the last shreds of hope as she whispered, 'They named the wrong person? It is Ryan?'

Clint shook his head. 'No. But the appointment wasn't to have been announced for a couple of weeks yet. The man Dan chose got over-anxious and let the news slip to a friend of his who works at the television station.'

'Then . . .' She swallowed hard, trying to reduce the awful lump in her throat. 'But you said he promised Ryan the job——'

'He didn't,' Clint said quickly. 'Dan never gave me his word, Brittany. If he had, he'd have kept it.'

'But he did give you his word about something,' she said quietly. 'You just said to him, "Dammit, Dan, you promised." ' She looked thoughtfully up at her father. 'What did Dan Curtis agree to do, Dad?'

He looked down at his hands, well kept, with closely trimmed nails. 'To consider Ryan for the job,' he said.

She stared at him for a long moment, then shook her head. 'I won't accept that,' she said. 'You were angry. You wouldn't have been, if his only promise was to keep Ryan in the running. So what was it, Dad?' Her quiet tone was more forceful than a scream could have been.

Clint shook his head sadly. 'I never could lie to your mother, either,' he said ruefully. 'She'd catch me out every time.'

Brittany just looked at him. Her whole body felt cold.

'Dan had already made his choice when I talked to him about Ryan,' he said wearily. 'He promised me that he wouldn't announce it for another couple of weeks—that the consumer advocate would be the last official appointment he made.'

'Why?' she whispered. 'Why did you do it, Dad?'

He sighed. 'To keep Ryan here,' he said finally.

'You knew?'

'Of course I knew. You're no actress, my love.'

'You manipulated us——' She was too furious to go on.

'I was only doing what you intended to do,' he pointed out. 'All I wanted was to give you two a chance to pick up your marriage again.'

'You made fools of us!' Her throat was so tight that her voice was barely a croak.

'I didn't intend to do anything of the sort. I thought

that, after a couple of years, you might both be over the loss of the baby and ready to go on with your lives, if someone just gave you the opportunity to realise that you still cared about each other.'

'Well, aren't you the little matchmaker?' She picked up a porcelain figurine that stood on the top of her desk, and hefted it in one hand, ready to dash it to the floor. Then, even though Ryan wasn't there to make her clean up the mess, she set it back carefully in its place with a trembling hand. 'Do me a favour, Dad,' she said politely.

'Britt, I'm sorry——'

'Don't give me any more help—I don't think I can stand it!'

He bowed his head. 'I'll call Felice over,' he said. 'She can sit with you.'

'It's her holiday,' Brittany said flatly. 'Let her enjoy what's left of it in peace.' She stalked up the stairs, shut herself into her room, and refused to come out.

She found some solace in her work. The week dragged by, without a break in the tension between her and her father, and without a word from Ryan.

I will not call him, she told herself. If I see him, I'll ask about the divorce. But I will not give him the slightest reason to think I'm seeking him out.

When the Foundation board assembled for its January meeting, though, Ryan's chair remained empty. Brittany sat through the formalities without hearing a word.

Lydia came to the office at the beginning of the second week, and sat down firmly beside Brittany's desk. 'And here I'll stay till I get some answers,' she said. 'I don't intend to be an interfering stepmother, Brittany, especially before the wedding—but this has gone far enough already.'

Brittany looked through her. 'Good, Lydia,' she said. 'I'm glad you don't plan to interfere.'

'Your father was wrong to do what he did. I told him in the beginning, when he and Dan first talked about it, that he'd regret it. Now he's terribly upset about this break between you. But you're frustrated about losing Ryan, and you're taking it out on Clint, Brittany. It's not fair to either of you.'

'And just what makes you think I'm frustrated about Ryan moving out? To tell you the truth, I'm delighted.'

'Right. You really look happy about it,' Lydia said drily. 'You've lost five pounds, you're pale, you look about as real as a ghost——'

'I'm feeling fine,' insisted Brittany.

'I don't believe it for a moment. Have you seen Dr Whittaker?' asked Lydia.

'Lydia, you are not helping matters!' Brittany shoved her chair back so violently that it almost tipped over. She strode across to the window and stood staring out over the city. The blanket of snow across the plaza beside First Federal's main entrance looked dirty grey to her eyes. The whole world looked grey these days, she thought.

The silence went unbroken for a few minutes, then Lydia sighed. 'I'm sorry,' she said. 'I love you, and I love Clint, and I hate to see you quarrelling this way.' She stood up. 'But you're right, my dear. It's none of my business. I won't bother you again.' There was a tiny, hurt quaver in her voice.

Brittany turned from the window, her arms outstretched. She let Lydia hold her close for a few moments. There was comfort in Lydia's embrace, and in the soft phrases she murmured into her ear. Then Brittany reached for the intercom on her desk, and asked her secretary to see if Mr Bridges could come in.

Clint arrived so quickly that Brittany almost suspected he'd been pacing the hall. 'I'm sorry, Dad,' she whispered. 'You were only doing what you thought was best for me.'

It ended up as a three-way hug, with all of them shedding a few tears. Clint dashed the telltale drops out of the corners of his eyes and said, 'Britt, Lydia and I have decided that we should postpone our wedding till you're feeling better.'

'Why?' She was honestly startled, and then she realised that a few months ago she would have thought it Clint's duty to give up his own plans for her sake. How much she had grown up in these last few weeks! she thought.

'We just don't think you should be alone,' Lydia explained.

Brittany started to laugh. 'Alone?' she repeated. 'In that house? It would be a miracle. No, you're going ahead with your plans. I'll be all right, really I will, and I'll recover sooner if I don't have someone hovering around asking how I feel!'

Eventually they yielded, and by the time they left her office, Brittany was even starting to feel just a little anticipation at the idea of a wedding in the house.

Then she remembered that after the newlyweds came back from Florida, her father would move into Lydia's house, and Brittany would again be alone in the Castle.

Alone, and lonely, she thought. Surrounded by servants, without a friend to count on.

'I'm going home,' she told her secretary. She didn't wait for an answer.

Eric Rhodes caught up with her in the hallway. 'Brittany!' he called.

She stopped reluctantly, put her briefcase down, and leaned against the nearest wall. 'Hello, Eric,' she said, determined to be cheerful, even though her stomach was churning. She had told Lydia that she was fine, but it was far from the truth; she hadn't felt worse in her life. 'I haven't seen much of you in the last couple of weeks.'

He laughed. 'No, but the worst is over now. I've had a time getting the mess straightened out after I'd got rid of my problem clerk.'

Brittany felt a little guilty. Dr Whittaker had asked more than once if she had reviewed that folder yet. It was still in her briefcase; Brittany had glanced at it several times, but she hadn't had the energy to struggle through the information. If Eric, who knew the department and the computer, hadn't been able to find a problem, how was she supposed to know where to look?

'Is it all straightened out?' she asked.

'Finally. The woman seems to have had a grudge against the bank, as well as me.'

'I see.' Funny, that she had fooled Sara Whittaker, Brittany thought.

'Are you going home already?' asked Eric.

'Yes. I'm so tired of the regular routine that I thought I'd work at home this afternoon.'

'You don't look tired. I'd have said you look much better than when your husband was hanging around. I was hoping you'd feel up to going to a concert with me tonight.'

She forced a smile. 'Sorry, Eric.' She stooped to pick up the briefcase, and Eric took it out of her hand.

'What have you got in this thing?' he joked, hefting it with a bit of effort. 'Dynamite?'

'Just files,' she said. 'Paper is heavy.'

He walked her down to the lobby. 'I'm so glad you got rid of the husband,' he confided. 'If we're not going to the concert, I'll drop over tonight, if I may.'

Though he had asked permission, the assumption in his voice was that he would be not only welcome, but eagerly awaited. Brittany was irritated.

'Not tonight,' she said coolly.

Eric smiled. 'Oh, come on, Brittany! It's a modern world, after all, and this time everybody knows you're going to divorce the great Mr Masters. We don't have to play games any more. They're all on our side.'

She was speechless. After all the times she had tried to disillusion him, he was still convinced she would fall into his hands like a ripe peach. Eric was charming, she had to admit. But how could any woman who had lived with Ryan turn to this man instead?

Thinking that way leads to trouble, she reminded herself. The Rolls was at the door, blocking the traffic, so she merely said, 'Not tonight, Eric,' and resolved that she would straighten out his mistaken thinking at the first opportunity.

Eric just smiled and blew her a kiss, which she ignored. 'Take me home, Jackson,' she said, and sank back into the soft leather with a tired sigh.

Peters took her coat and her briefcase, and Brittany climbed the stairs to her bedroom to change from the tweed suit to something more comfortable. Felice was singing as she sorted and straightened the contents of drawers in Brittany's dressing room. 'Oh,' she exclaimed, startled, when Brittany came in. 'I wasn't expecting you, madam——'

'Don't stop, Felice. I like to hear you sing—it's much better than the old silence.'

Felice giggled. 'It is, isn't it? It's much nicer to work for you now, madam.' She started to sing again, a soft love song.

Brittany's hands clenched against the pain that the tender words brought to her. She doesn't realise, she told herself. Felice didn't even think about it.

The maid turned from the closet and spotted Brittany's white knuckles. 'I'm sorry,' she whispered. 'I never thought——'

Brittany tried to smile.

'You love him very much, don't you?' asked Felice quietly.

Brittany didn't try to answer. She changed as quickly as she could, and went back downstairs.

But the Castle was quiet, and there was too much time to think. She found herself longing for someone to keep her company. Even Jeff had been entertaining, she thought, with his computer proficiency and his never-ending conversation. But since Ryan had left the Castle, Jeff had not been back either.

Was he hanging around Ryan's new apartment by now? Or was Ryan still sleeping on the couch in his office? She hoped not; he needed his sleep.

She sighed and decided not to think about it any more. There was always work to be done; it would be far better for her to concentrate on that.

She emptied her briefcase on to the desk. The files made a huge stack, and the top one slid off, its contents splattering on to the floor, before she could catch it. She swore and bent to pick it up.

It was the folder Sara Whittaker had passed on to her. 'I should have just given it to Eric today,' she muttered. 'Instead, I'm still hauling it around. That takes brains, Brittany.' She picked up a chart. The woman was compulsively neat, that was certain, she told herself. Who else would have drawn a bar graph illustrating the amount of toilet paper that First Federal had purchased over the last five years?

And who else would have noticed that the quantity had nearly doubled in the last few months?

'Fascinating,' muttered Brittany. Her interest piqued, she sat down with the folder and spread the contents out on a table.

Twenty minutes later, she pushed the papers aside and stared into space, biting her lip. For the first time in two weeks, her brain seemed to be functioning at full power. There was no doubt about it, she thought: supplies were disappearing left and right, supplies that First Federal had ordered and paid for. And because it had been such tiny items as disposable towels, paper clips, and soap, no one had taken it seriously.

No one except the single clerk, who had gone on a kind of quest to find the missing supplies—'And was fired for her efforts,' Brittany thought.

She tapped a pencil against the folder. Why couldn't Eric find the problem? she wondered. It had been obvious enough to her.

And it must have been obvious to Eric as well, she thought. No one who knew the computer system as well as he did could have been fooled. Which left only one answer: Eric knew all about the disappearing supplies, and he had fired the clerk to cover up the scheme.

There was one way to tell for sure, she thought. She'd check the computer itself.

Half an hour later she admitted defeat. The password listed in her handbook got her nowhere; he must have installed a new security system. She sat there and stared at the screen. Then she called Jeff and asked if he could come over.

He arrived, after a stop in the kitchen, with a handful of chocolate-chip cookies and a glass of milk. 'After-school snack,' he pointed out. 'Want a cookie?'

Brittany bit her lip to keep from smiling at his generosity. It was, after all, her kitchen that had supplied the cookies! When she told him what she wanted, he shook his head. 'Can't,' he said briefly. 'I promised Ryan I'd never break into a computer again.'

'You're not breaking in, exactly,' she argued. 'You have my permission.'

They argued for a little while, but she could see that Jeff was weakening. The sheer challenge was wearing him down.

Brittany absentmindedly picked up a cookie. Not bad, she decided as she bit into it. She didn't realise that it was the first thing she had eaten all day.

'What if I hurt it?' queried Jeff. 'Hey, that was the last cookie!'

'Sorry. If there's any damage done to the computer or the bank's records, I'll be responsible.'

He eyed her. 'And you'll explain it to Ryan?'

'Scout's honour.' Brittany crossed her fingers behind her back and hoped that would never be necessary.

'Then go get me some more cookies,' he ordered. 'I can't work on an empty stomach.'

She went in search of Peters, and by the time he had brought in the tea tray and a platter of still-steaming cookies, Jeff was leaning back in his chair, hands clasped behind his head, watching columns of numbers scroll by on the screen.

She leaned over his shoulder. 'How did you do that?' she demanded.

'Nothing to it,' Jeff told her. There was disgust in his voice. 'And that guy thinks he knows all about computers?'

Brittany was watching the numbers go by. Somewhere in there, she was sure, was the answer—where were those supplies disappearing to? 'Can you make it print all of those things?' she asked.

'Sure.' He tapped a few keys, and the printer clattered into action. Then he propped his feet up on the edge of the desk and dug into the plate of cookies. 'You see, it's very simple,' he began.

'Right. It certainly looks simple. Jeff, would you like a job securing our computers from people just like you?'

'Hackers is the usual term,' he said comfortably, through a cookie. 'Besides, most people wouldn't get in as easily as I did.'

'Thank heaven!'

'Because you'd already tied the computer into the main system before I got here. That's where most of the security is. But if you'd like to make a bet on whether I could break in from scratch——'

'No, thanks.' Brittany started to pick up the papers that had been in the clerk's folder. She stopped at a thick document printed on computer paper. It was the same list that the printer was now producing. 'We went to all that work just to get another copy of something we already had?' she wailed.

Jeff shrugged. 'I just produced what you told me to. I'd better go do my homework.'

'Thanks, Jeff,' she said, and gave him a hug. 'Come over any time you want.'

'I thought you didn't want me hanging around any more, now that Ryan——' He hung his head.

'To tell the truth,' Brittany admitted, 'I've kind of missed you.'

He gave her a lopsided grin. 'In that case, can I do my homework here?'

They worked in companionable silence for the next hour. Peters brought in a fresh pot of tea, stared thoughtfully at the cookie in Brittany's hand for an instant, and returned a few minutes later with a plate of tiny sandwiches which he put unobtrusively at her elbow.

By that time, she had descended to comparing the clerk's list of bills paid, item by item, with the one the computer had spat out this afternoon. And the two, she quickly realised, had little in common. The amounts were different. The notes of which supplies had been purchased were different. Even the names of the companies were different. Only the totals at the end of each page added up the same.

If I were trying to steal from my employer, she asked herself, how would I do it? Just how could Eric hide all those supplies, anyway? And where was he selling them?

Because it had to be Eric, she told herself. At the very least, he was covering up the scheme, but she was fairly certain he was the genius behind it as well. It was Eric, after all, who had volunteered to run that department. It was Eric who had set up the computer system to handle it—and set it up very neatly, she realised now, to cover up his own sideline. If it hadn't been for one alert and persistent clerk, his game could have gone on for ever.

She made a list, idly, of the companies that were on the first list but not on the second. There were half a dozen of them. She stared at the list for a few minutes, as if the mere names would answer her question. How would I have done it? she asked herself. The answer was breathtakingly simple.

I wouldn't bother with stealing supplies, she told herself. I'd write up invoices from imaginary companies, then pay the bills and deposit the money to my account.

A few minutes with the telephone directory confirmed her suspicions. There were companies with similar names in the book, but none of the ones on her list were there at all.

No wonder no one could find all the excess stationery and paper towels! she thought. None of that stuff ever existed—but we certainly paid for it. She tossed her pencil down with a sigh of relief.

Jeff asked, 'Can I have one of those sandwiches?'

'Sure.' Brittany reached for the plate. 'Oh—I'm sorry, Jeff. I must have eaten them all.'

He grinned, 'Well, that's a fine thing to do to a guest!'

She could hardly believe it herself. She had had no appetite for days.

'Hey, Peters!' called Jeff. 'Mrs Masters ate all the sandwiches. Are there any more?'

The butler looked approving. 'I'm glad to see you're feeling better, madam,' he said softly, as he replaced the empty plate with a full one.

So am I, Brittany thought. For the first time in two weeks, she felt as if there was some hope after all, and some reason to go on struggling against the awful pain in her heart.

The wedding went off without a snag. It was simple, quiet, plain, just Clint and Lydia, the judge who married them, Brittany, a handful of guests, and an empty place where Ryan should have been. Brittany was so busy thinking about the empty place that she scarcely heard the ceremony.

'I still think I should have given you a reception,' she said as she presided at dinner that night.

Clint shook his head. 'We'll coerce you into a garden party next summer,' he said. 'Frankly, I'm looking forward to a warm climate so much that you couldn't get me to stay around here another day!'

Lydia frowned a little. 'But if Brittany needs us——'

'Yes, of course.' Clint's forehead was wrinkled. 'I heard that Eric made a nasty scene in your office yesterday before he left.'

'That's right.' Brittany shivered a little as she thought about it.

It had taken two weeks for the auditors to collect all the evidence, but Brittany's intuitive reasoning had proved correct. Thousands of dollars were missing, funnelled through non-existent supply companies, into Eric's accounts, and from there to his stockbroker. Eric, it seemed, had been taking an occasional expensive flyer in the stock market.

'How did you find out about the stock market?' she asked curiously. 'He must have been very careful about it.'

Clint looked ever so slightly guilty. 'From Ryan,' he admitted. 'I don't quite know what made him suspicious, but he'd set that private detective of his on to Eric. He didn't know where the money was coming from, of course, but he soon found out that Eric was spending considerably more than his salary.'

'And he didn't tell me?'

'Would you have listened?' Clint asked dryly. 'Besides, he was only able to confirm it last week, and he called me right away. He didn't want you to be hurt.'

Brittany bit her lip and didn't answer.

When Clint and the auditors had faced Eric with the evidence, he had bluffed and blustered. Brittany hadn't been there, but she'd heard it all from Eric, later.

He'd been calm and composed when he first came to talk to her, with only the slightest wild look in his eyes. 'They offered me a deal,' he told her. 'If I resign, your father won't prosecute.'

Brittany herself had agreed to that course of action, but only under pressure. The reputation of the bank was at stake, Clint had told her. If word leaked out that First Federal had an embezzler, the public's confidence in the bank would be shaken. She knew that he was right, and yet it seemed unfair that Eric's only punishment was to lose his job.

'And what options do you have?' she had asked Eric wryly.

He dropped into a chair beside her desk. 'If you were to talk to your father——' he began.

'Eric, it wouldn't change things.'

'But he doesn't know how we feel about each other! If he knew, he wouldn't fire me——'

'What would you suggest he do? Turn over the trust accounts to you?'

The sarcasm in her tone began to register with him. 'Brittany——' he whimpered.

'And as for how we feel about each other, Eric,' she went on, 'I've never given you any reason to think that I cared for you except as a friend. Anything more than that, you've conjured up out of your own wishful thinking.'

'You're everything I've ever wanted in a wife, Brittany. You're beautiful, intelligent——'

'Rich,' she added pointedly.

He looked hurt. 'You think I'm a fortune-hunter, only interested in your money, don't you? That's not so, Brittany. I'm not like Masters——'

How dared he compare himself with Ryan? 'Out!' she snapped. 'Get out of my office.'

'Brittany! If you'd just talk to your father——'

'I already have, Eric.' He looked relieved. 'I told him you should go to prison for what you've done. Take the deal, Eric. It's all you're going to get.'

He had gone, then. He had looked six inches shorter, and ten years older. He had left First Federal that morning, and the clerk he had fired was already back at work, as the new head of the department. It would take her weeks to patch up the damage Eric had done as he tried to cover his tracks.

Brittany sighed. Had she led him on, encouraged him to believe that she might marry him one day? In his view, he had just been taking an advance on the money that would come to him some day. Had she caused him to think that way?

No, she told herself. She'd been blind not to see through him sooner, and foolish not to have told him at the start that she could never care for him. But she was not to blame for what had happened.

'Well, Brittany?' asked Clint. 'Do you need us to stay here? It's not too late to change our plans.'

She finished off her dessert. She was actually hungry these days, she thought. 'Don't be silly,' she said. 'Give up your honeymoon because Eric was caught with his fingers in the till?' It wasn't that, of course, and she knew it. But she forced herself to laugh, and to pretend that she was all right. She saw no need for them to suffer the consequences of her foolishness.

They left soon after that, for their first night in their new home. She wouldn't see them again till they returned from Florida in a few weeks.

Brittany retreated to her sitting room. You shouldn't have finished off that dessert, she told herself. Indigestion is a fearful thing to have at this hour of the night. It was foolish, she thought, but she kept doing the same thing over and over. She felt hungry, so she ate. Then the indigestion came, and she soothed it with hot tea. Then she would feel hungry again.

She was glad Lydia had gone home. Lydia would have told her to see Dr Whittaker.

Not a bad idea at that, Brittany told herself, as a particularly harsh pain racked her. Not that there's anything physically wrong, she added. If I'd just forget about Ryan, this upset stomach would fix itself in a hurry.

But wanting to forget Ryan, and doing it, were two different things.

CHAPTER ELEVEN

SARA WHITTAKER chewed on her pencil and looked puzzled. 'You may be right,' she said. 'It could be simply a reaction to stress. Our bodies do funny things sometimes, and heaven knows you've been under enough pressure lately. But it's also possible that you're developing an ulcer. Of course I can't diagnose that for certain without more tests. I think you should go over to the hospital——'

Brittany glanced at the clock. 'I can't,' she said. 'I have a Foundation board meeting in ten minutes.'

Sara groaned. 'Don't you ever miss one of those things?'

Certainly not this one, Brittany wanted to say. I haven't seen Ryan in more than a month. He might not come today, or he might not want to talk to me. But in case he does, I'm going to be there.

Sara waved a hand. 'All right. But come back here when the meeting is over.'

'I can't spend all day down here while you do research on me, you know. I'm certain there's nothing physically wrong——'

'Stop quibbling and go to your meeting. You can come back and argue about it later.' Sara picked up her clipboard and walked out.

Brittany dropped the examination gown on to a chair and got dressed faster than ever before in her life. But she was still two minutes late to the board meeting, and the chairman was rapping the gavel when she reached her chair, breathless.

Ryan didn't seem to notice. In the old days, she

165

thought, he would have had an acidly humorous comment, and she would have wanted to hit him with something. She certainly would never have expected that some day she would feel almost lonely for those smart remarks he used to make. Today, she might as well have been invisible for all the attention he paid to her.

And what did you expect, she asked herself, from a man who told you when he left that you were driving him crazy? She studied him out of the corner of her eye, willing herself to see some change. Was he thinner, perhaps? Or was there just a tinge of white hair at his temples?

Honesty forced her to give up the search. Nothing about him had changed; she could find no evidence that he missed her or regretted his decision to leave. That's because he doesn't regret it, she told herself firmly. The sooner you recognize that fact, the better it will be for everyone.

She doodled her name on the legal pad that lay on the table in front of her, and half-listened to the proceedings. She wasn't much good as a director these days, she thought. Perhaps she should resign from the Foundation altogether, and let Clint and the chairman appoint someone else.

No, she told herself, the truth was, it wouldn't be the Foundation that she would be trying to escape from. She would be running away from Ryan, and that was silly. What was the good in running from someone who had no desire to follow?

'You all have the information on the grants that we'll be considering today,' the chairman said. 'I assume that you have reviewed them.'

Brittany had—in the elevator on her way to the meeting. She reached for the folder of notes in her briefcase, and her hand brushed Ryan's as he bent to pick up the pen he'd dropped. 'Sorry,' she said quickly, pulling away from the momentary contact.

His jaw tightened. He didn't reply, just chased the errant pen down and settled back into his chair. As far away from me as he can possibly get, Brittany thought miserably.

'We'll take the applications up in order,' the chairman said. 'The investigating committee's report is attached to each application. The first one is——'

'Excuse me, Mr Chairman.' Ryan leaned forward. 'I missed last month's meeting, and I can't tell from the minutes whether the treasurer was successful in convincing Mrs Masters that the Foundation isn't going to be bankrupt before the end of the fiscal year.'

'And what does that have to do with this month's applications?' Brittany turned to face him.

He glanced at her, then looked away as if the sight of her was painful. 'I just wanted to know if a negative vote from you will mean that you disagree with the application, or if it reflects a general disapproval of spending money at all.'

Brittany started to do a slow burn. 'That's an unfair question! No matter how I answer it, I come out as either a fool or a miser.'

Brown eyes lifted from the folder of applications on the table in front of him. 'You said it, I didn't,' he murmured.

The chairman cleared his throat. 'Let's take up the first application,' he said.

The two of them split neatly on every issue. 'That's ridiculous,' Ryan protested once, about halfway through the list. 'What grounds can you possibly have for refusing to fund that experiment?'

'First,' said Brittany, 'he's trying to do something that is impossible. Second——'

'How do you know it's impossible?' Ryan asked gently.

'Second,' Brittany repeated, 'there is no practical market.'

'Of course there isn't,' he agreed. 'There wasn't a practical market for oil when it was first discovered, either, but look what's happened to it since.'

'Mr Chairman,' she snapped, goaded beyond all endurance, 'there is no point in this. I take exception to being attacked for voting my conscience, which is the only requirement of a member of this board. Would you please instruct Mr Masters to stop heckling me?'

'Mr Chairman,' Ryan returned, 'I'm sorry if the lady feels persecuted. Perhaps she's simply out of tune with the rest of the board. I had no intention of heckling her, however.' He actually sounded sorry, which Brittany didn't believe for a moment.

After that, though, he said no more. They cast their votes without additional comment, and actually agreed on a couple of applications, which sent Ryan's eyebrows skyward. Brittany ignored him as best she could. He was watching her very closely, she thought, and wondered uneasily what he'd seen that had caught his attention.

The meeting ended. Brittany was gathering up her papers when Ryan said quietly, 'We need to talk, Brittany. May I buy you lunch?'

The very thought of sitting across the table from him, eating anything at all, was enough to make her feel ill. She shook her head. 'I have a date,' she said flatly.

'With Eric, I suppose.'

'Didn't Jeff tell you? Or Dad?' Then she bit her tongue, regretting that she'd said anything at all.

'Tell me what?'

'Eric isn't at First Federal any more.' She finished loading her briefcase.

'So he did have his fingers in the till!' Before she could comment, he added, 'That wouldn't keep you from having lunch with him, of course, if you were determined. What about dinner tonight?'

Her nerves, stretched by tension and illness, had reached the limit. 'Let's cut out the props and the pretence, all right? Just send me the papers, Ryan.'

He stared down at her for a long moment. 'All right,' he said. 'If that's the way you want it.' He turned towards the door.

It isn't, she wanted to say. She wanted to run after him and beg him to come back.

Why? she thought. Why did I have to fall in love wr..1 a man who's so nearly my opposite? Why couldn't I have chosen someone like me, who saw things the way I do?

Because, she knew, most of the things that most irritated her about Ryan were outgrowths of his nature— sensitive, caring, tender—the very thing that had attracted her in the first place. She had felt that tenderness once, directed towards her. There had been a hint of it again, when he had asked her to lunch. And she had killed it, deliberately and coldly.

At least it's over, she told herself, and went back to the executive floor, planning to barricade herself in her office.

Sara Whittaker was waiting for her. 'I didn't think you'd come back to the clinic,' she said.

'Why should I? You can't do anything for me.'

'Have you no faith in modern medicine? I can even promise you a cure. The whole syndrome will run its course in a matter of weeks.'

'A few weeks of this?' Brittany's voice trailed off to a whisper. 'And you can't do anything about it?'

'It won't be this bad all the time, of course. The indigestion will come and go for a while before it disappears.' She smiled. 'You had me fooled for a little while! I'm not used to seeing morning sickness that never occurs in the morning. Running a pregnancy test was an afterthought—which just goes to show that doctors never reach the point of knowing everything.'

Brittany sat down in the nearest chair. 'Oh, my God!' she muttered.

'Last time we talked about it, having a baby seemed to be your fondest wish,' Sara observed. 'Have you changed your mind?'

'No. Yes!' A baby? Now I really feel sick, Britt thought. It was the one thing that had never occurred to her, and it should have been obvious.

Sara looked disappointed. 'It's your choice, of course,' she shrugged. 'For someone in your position, there are always alternatives.' She stood up. 'You'll need to see a good obstetrician right away—assuming that you decide to have the baby. Let me know.'

Could she have her baby alone? Raise a child alone? A few weeks ago, Brittany reminded herself, there had been no doubt in her mind at all about her fitness as a parent; now the mere idea frightened her. She tried to take her mind off the question. 'An obstetrician?' she asked. 'Isn't it a little early for that?'

'Not with your history,' Sara Whittaker said bluntly. 'I'm not terribly concerned about another miscarriage, but we'd better not take chances. We don't want to lose this baby, too.'

For a few moments, Brittany had actually forgotten about the miscarriage. Her breath seemed to catch, and fear raked over her. The instantaneous reaction told her one thing—she would fight all the way, if that was what it took, to save this baby. Instinctively, she put one hand protectively over her abdomen.

It was the only answer Sara Whittaker needed. 'Good,' she said. 'I hoped you'd feel that way. I brought a pre-natal diet for you to follow, starting right now.' She tossed a pamphlet down on the desk. 'Drink plenty of milk; it will help soothe your stomach. And there are things we can give you to ease the nausea.'

'Not if they might hurt the baby.' It was automatic.

Sara smiled. 'That's a good girl! And I'll make an appointment for you with the best specialist in town.'

'Won't you take care of me?' Brittany's voice was small. She felt as if she was being deserted. 'You told me once that you'd planned to be an obstetrician.'

Sara smiled. 'You just try to get rid of me!' she said. 'I have every intention of being there when this baby makes a grand entrance. But I can't stay with you for the next seven months. I have other patients—and I have to get back to them.' She waved from the door.

Brittany sank into her chair. Her head was spinning. Now it all seemed so obvious. After all, she'd been pregnant before, and yet it was really no surprise that she hadn't recognised this illness. 'I thought I knew what morning sickness was,' she laughed ruefully. She'd had a little mild discomfort a time or two, and moaned about how miserable she was. But it had been nothing like this.

This baby, she told herself, apparently wanted all her attention already. 'You're going to be difficult,' she accused. 'Just like your father——'

The wave of pain was like a deluge over her. She wasn't even sure if it was physical or emotional; all that she knew was how badly she hurt.

I'll have to tell Ryan, she thought. There was no escaping that. Even if there was a way to conceal her pregnancy from him, and prevent the grapevine from carrying the news, there was the matter of the divorce to consider. Their child would have to be part of that. 'Just like another piece of property,' she told herself.

Better get it over with, she thought, and picked up the telephone before she could change her mind.

'This is Mrs Masters,' she told the woman who answered the phone at the legal clinic. 'I'd like to speak to my husband, please.'

,I'm sorry, Mr Masters isn't here at the moment.'

A slightly different excuse, she thought. Not the old standard—he's in court. Well, perhaps it was true this time; he might have simply gone out to lunch after all. 'Thank you, Mary,' she said.

'Ma'am? I'm afraid you're mistaken. Miss Anderson isn't working here any more. May I take a message for Mr Masters?'

Brittany hesitated. 'No, no message.' She cradled the telephone gently. Odd, she thought, that Mary Anderson had moved on; Brittany would have sworn that the woman would finish out her days working for Ryan.

Suddenly she was unbearably tired. She had eaten very little for breakfast, and no lunch at all. There was no point in trying to work when all she wanted to do was go home.

'It's a good thing Dad isn't here,' she told herself. 'I haven't worked a full day all week. He'd fire me for laziness!'

Like heck, she added. He'll be delighted at the news.

Peters hovered over her, making sure her lunch was perfect. Ryan had been right, she thought: the last few days, since Clint had been gone, had made her realise that dining in state, alone, was sort of silly. She pushed her chair back and smiled up at Peters. 'That was lovely,' she said. 'Thank you.'

It was amazing, she thought, what an effect the simple words had on him. He seemed to glow just a little. 'I'll tell the cook,' he said. 'Are you certain you won't have dessert? She has a lovely cream puff for you.'

Brittany shook her head. 'Right now, all I want is a nap,' she said. She stopped in the doorway. 'Peters, would you bring me a glass of milk, please?'

There was a moment of dead silence; Peters had even stopped clearing the table. 'Milk, madam?' he echoed, as if she had ordered something deadly.

'I know I never drink the stuff,' Brittany agreed. 'Nevertheless——'

'I see,' said Peters, and Brittany thought wryly that he probably saw a great deal too much. 'Milk it is, madam.'

The Christmas tree was long gone, but she found herself staring at the bay window in the drawing room where it had stood. It had been a symbol of new hope this year, she thought. And, in the end, it had been nothing more than another false start.

A bit of bright red peeped out from under the edge of the loveseat, a jarring note in the peach and blue room. She bent over to see what it was.

The cheap little Mexican straw bell with its bedraggled red ribbon lay forlornly on the carpet, deserted there and left behind when the rest of the decorations had been put away. Somehow it had escaped the housekeeper's eagle eye. Brittany picked it up, cradling it carefully in her palm, and carried it with her into the sitting room. She set it on the mantel, carefully. It would never decorate a tree again, she thought. She would put it away, very carefully. And some day she would tell her son or daughter about the day Ryan had bought it for her. It would be important for the child to know that once they had cared for each other.

The glass of milk that Peters brought sent her off to sleep. Felice tiptoed into the sitting room a little later, with a blanket. When Brittany opened her eyes, the maid said softly, 'I didn't mean to disturb you, madam, but I was afraid you'd be cold.'

Brittany closed her eyes and sighed. It had been such a pleasant dream, she thought, and a tear slipped down her cheek. Ryan had been there with her, in her dream. It had been he who had tucked the blanket close around her and the baby . . .

I love my baby, she thought. Or at least I will—it's a little hard to get attached to a human being who's no larger, at the moment, than my thumb. But what I really want is my baby's father.

And why not? she thought. Perhaps, if I fight for him . . . But she was too tired to think about it just then, so she dropped off to sleep again instead. Tomorrow would be time enough to fight.

She roused slowly, feeling as if she was pushing her way out of a fog. She must have slept for hours, she thought. Why hadn't they awakened her?

She sat up, suddenly panicky at the silence in the house. Was everyone gone?

'Don't get up suddenly,' a voice said from across the room. 'You'll be dizzy if you do.'

For a moment, she thought she was hearing things. 'Ryan?' she whispered.

He saw her shock, and must have thought it was anger. 'Don't blame Peters,' he said. 'He didn't let me in.'

'Then how——'

'I came in the back way. I never did return my key.'

'Why did you come?' Her voice was hoarse. She must still be half asleep, she thought. She wasn't sure what was real.

'You called my office,' he reminded her. 'I telephoned the bank, but your secretary said you weren't feeling well, and that you'd gone home early.'

'It wasn't urgent,' said Brittany. She sat up, with her feet curled up under her, and rearranged the blanket. No wonder the room was quiet, she thought; he had closed the carved double doors that led to the drawing room. 'Or did you have a reason for coming?'

He ignored the interruption. 'When I called here, Peters told me you'd eaten half your lunch and gone out like a light on the couch. It didn't sound like you.'

Brittany said stiffly, 'You certainly didn't need to come dashing over here to check on me.'

'It's quite obvious that you wish I'd go away. You don't

need to keep telling me.'

She bit her lip. 'Peters should know better than to give out information like that!'

'I am still your husband,' Ryan reminded her curtly. 'As long as you wear that ring, I have the right to ask about you.'

I should resent him saying that, she thought. Instead, the words seemed to snag at her heart. She pulled the gold band off her finger and flung it on to the coffee table, where it spun slowly for a few seconds. She watched it, feeling as if she was saying goodbye to a very precious part of her life.

Ryan had watched it too. He looked up in the silence, his eyes hard. 'So let's get down to business,' he said. 'You did say you wanted me to start the paperwork for the divorce. Here it is.' He tossed an envelope on to the table.

She looked at it for a long moment, then picked it up carefully, as if the documents might bite her.

'The preliminary papers are complete,' he said. 'All you have to do is sign the petition, and the divorce will be under way. The final documents will have to be completed, of course. I just jotted down some notes on a property settlement and all that sort of thing, for you to look over.'

Brittany swallowed hard. So much for her half-waking resolve to fight for him, she thought. She had told him to send her the papers; he was in such a hurry that he had delivered them in person. Well, she had known even in her sleep that it was foolish to dream of a reconciliation.

She paged through the documents, shuddering inwardly at the sight of her marriage reduced to cold legal phrases. 'Irreconcilable differences,' she saw. 'Irreparable breakdown of the marital relationship.' It hurt to see their disagreements reduced to black and white.

'I assumed you would want to be the one who actually

filed,' said Ryan.

She nodded, then set the document aside and went on to the pages of yellow legal paper, covered with his precise handwriting. It was the list of their assets, she saw, the things they had purchased together.

'There's some stock, too,' she said. 'Dad bought it in both our names.'

Ryan shrugged. 'Do as you like with it. It makes no difference to me.'

'You mean you trust the acquisitive banker to be fair about it?' It was said before she could stop herself.

He winced. 'Please, Brittany! Don't remind me of every foolish thing I ever said.'

She looked down the list. 'The Castle is half yours, too,' she reminded him. 'You've put it on the list of things I'm to keep.'

He looked around. 'I never seemed to belong here,' he said quietly. 'And I don't want any part of it now.'

It was like an epitaph. 'Nevertheless,' she said, 'I'll have it appraised, and pay you for your share.'

He smiled suddenly. 'I never thought I'd have a divorce case where the parties kept trying to give away assets!' he said.

The sudden twist of humour hurt her almost worse than all the rest. It brought back the beautiful early days, when there were still things to laugh about, before Diana Winslow and the miscarriage had got in the way. Why should he turn the money down? she wondered. This, at least, was his, without question. The Castle had been her father's gift to both of them.

'If that's all,' said Ryan, 'you just sign there on the back page. I'll file it with the court tomorrow.'

Brittany turned back to the first page. 'It's not quite all,' she said.

She saw his jaw tighten. 'What else do you want?' he asked acidly. 'Alimony? If so, remember you can't get much from me—I can't afford to buy your toothpaste, Brittany.'

She flinched under his sharp words. How can I tell him about the baby now? she thought. How can I find the words, when we're arguing about stupid things like this, to tell him that in those few mad, magic nights we made a new life?

Under the blanket, her hand went protectively to her abdomen. It shouldn't be like this, she thought. This news should be greeted with joy, not with horror and argument.

We've cheated you, my child, she wanted to say. We've foolishly thrown away your right to have two parents.

I can't tell him, now, she thought. In a few weeks, when the legal proceedings were under way, perhaps the bitterness would have died down, and they could at least be human about it, and decide how they could work it out. She would not give the baby up, of course. She wondered if Ryan would even want to see his child.

She knew, of course, that she had only postponed the inevitable, but relief swept over her as she decided she did not have to form those difficult words right now. 'Maybe I should be offering you alimony,' she said quietly. 'I'll at least pay your regular rates for your work——'

'Don't try it.' Underneath the easy tone, it sounded like a threat. 'When will you learn, Brittany, that money can't buy peace of mind?'

'I know it,' she said. It was almost a whisper. 'What will you do, Ryan?' she asked.

He seemed surprised that she cared enough to ask. 'I'll stay at the clinic,' he told her. 'It seems to be what I'm supposed to do with my life.'

'I'm sorry about the job,' she said. 'I did the best I could to get it for you.'

His mouth twisted just a little. 'I know,' he said. 'You made it very obvious.'

Why did he sound angry? she wondered. He had asked for her help, after all.

'What was it that you wanted to change in the petition?' he asked, picking up the document.

'Nothing,' she said. 'It's fine as it is.' They could always add to it, later, the fact that there was a child to be considered.

'Then there's no point in putting it off, is there?' There was no arguing with that quiet logic. He reached into his breast pocket and handed her a pen.

The metal case was warm from his body. She leaned forward and spread the paper out on the coffee table. The pen seemed to burn her hand.

Then something snapped, deep inside her. 'I won't,' she said, in a harsh whisper. 'I won't!'

'What?' Ryan was astounded. 'If you mean you want another attorney to read it before you sign, let me assure you that it's as fair as I can make it——'

'I will not sign it!' she said again, on a rising note of panic. The pen was still clenched in her hand. She was afraid to keep holding it, so she threw it, as hard as she could, across the room.

'What the devil——' He stared at her for a moment, as if she had suddenly turned into a wild animal, then he shrugged. 'I don't know what's the matter with you, Brittany,' he said finally. 'Whenever you decide to be reasonable, call me.'

'Take this with you,' she said. Her hands trembled as she folded the petition and thrust it at him. 'You can rewrite it, and file it yourself if you like. But I won't!'

He stood there, looking blank and stunned, with the document in his hand. 'Brittany?' he said at last. It was a bare whisper.

Now you've done it, she thought. You've made a first-class fool of yourself this time. You've sacrificed your pride, and stripped your soul naked——

And what difference could it make if she told him the truth? she asked herself. He deserved to see the pain he had caused. She wanted him to see how much she had changed, how hard she had tried to please him. And then, when he walked away, at least he wouldn't be so damned self-righteous any more!

She was crying, harsh, racking sobs that threatened to choke her. 'Damn you, Ryan Masters!' she exclaimed. 'You wanted me to be a woman instead of a plastic doll. Now see what you've done to me! You've broken me. I never knew it was possible to hurt so much, but you've taught me how! You've taken everything that was the best of me, and then thrown it aside and told me it wasn't good enough.' She gasped for breath, and said softly, 'And God help me, I'm trying one more time to buy you—because I still love you.'

Ryan was like a statue in the centre of the floor.

She stood up, slowly, her hands clenched at her sides. 'Would you like to see me beg?' she asked. 'I will. Stay with me, Ryan. Take whatever you want, whatever I can give you. Just let me pretend that you care for me——' Her foot caught in the corner of the blanket, and she stumbled.

'Brittany!' He caught her, and for an instant her head rested against his shoulder. She closed her eyes to drink in the sweet ecstasy of being there, with his heart beating beneath her cheek.

When he pushed her gently away, she gasped, 'No—please! Just hold me for a little while——'

He held her away from him. 'Brittany, look at me,' he demanded.

She opened her eyes, then, and looked up into stern brown ones.

'I am not for sale,' he said.

She sniffed, hiccuped once, swallowed hard. 'I know,' she said miserably. 'I'm sorry. I did it again, didn't I— that dreadful streak of selfishness. But all I want is for you to be happy. That's the truth, Ryan.'

He brushed a wet lock of hair back from her cheek. The tender gesture brought fresh tears to her eyes. He bent his head to kiss them away, and she thought, I could die right here in his arms, when he's being kind to me.

'Just as long as you realise that you don't own me,' he said. 'You will never own me.' It didn't even sound like his voice, somehow, but before she had time to analyse it, he was kissing her with a frantic hunger that threatened to suffocate them both.

When he finally released her, she was trembling. 'Please,' she whispered, 'don't ever let me go again.'

He did, but just long enough to lead her across the room and pull her down on his lap in a big chair. Brittany put her head on his shoulder. 'I'll do anything you want, Ryan,' she said, 'as long as you'll stay with me. A job at the bank—Dad said you could have whatever you wanted——'

'Absolutely not!' His voice was harsh. 'I will never work for First Federal, Brittany. Is that plain enough for you? You wanted me there, and I wanted to please you. But I couldn't force myself to do it. Clint knew that from the beginning.'

She nodded. She didn't understand, but she believed him. 'Whatever you want, Ryan. But there's just one thing.'

He looked down at her with doubt in his eyes. 'Somehow I thought there'd be a snag. What is it?'

'Will you promise me to do your best to keep the affairs from becoming public? That's all I ask,' she added hurriedly, for she had felt every muscle in his body tighten.

'What does that mean? What affairs?'

'You didn't think I knew, did you?' She was almost proud of herself. She had succeeded in concealing that hurt, after all. 'I've known for ages, since right after I lost the baby.' The baby, she thought; I still haven't told him about the baby. 'Mary Anderson came to see me, and told me about Diana.'

'What in hell did she tell you?' His voice was tight.

Why was he asking? she wondered. So he would know how much he would have to admit to? She told him, briefly. She had no trouble remembering; Mary Anderson's words were engraved on her memory.

'So that's what she was babbling about.' He seemed to be talking to himself.

'What do you mean? Who?'

He sighed. 'Mary hasn't been doing her job lately. I called her in a couple of weeks ago to warn her, and she told me that it didn't matter, that she knew when I left you again that sooner or later I'd discover that it was her that I really loved. I told her there was no chance of that, and she started to scream at me that I might as well give up on you because she'd told you all about me—Oh, God. To think that one jealous woman could cause so much trouble!'

'It doesn't matter, Ryan.' Brittany was breathless as she tried to reassure him. 'I understand that I wasn't much of a wife to you then. I don't blame you for turning to Diana. And I won't be jealous any more——'

He shook her gently. 'Not you, dammit,' he said gently. 'Mary. Don't you see, Brittany? She knew you'd never believe that I preferred her to you, so she spun you a tale about Diana. She made it up, to get you to throw me out.' He looked down at her sadly. 'Which is exactly what you did.'

'But she couldn't have made it up!'

'Not out of whole cloth, perhaps. As I recall, I was seeing quite a bit of Diana. But I wasn't sleeping with

her, Brittany. You're the only woman I've ever wanted to
have in my bed.' His voice was husky.

She wanted to believe him. It was hard not to, with his
hands warm against her skin.

'I'm telling the truth, Brittany. I swear on my life that I
never had an affair with Diana. Or anyone else, either.'
There was a harsh undercurrent in his voice, a bitter
undercurrent.

She looked up at him, and remembered the look in
Mary Anderson's eyes that day. She had thought at the
time that the woman was relieved that Brittany
understood. But instead it had been delight. 'I fell for it,'
she whispered. 'If I'd only told you then what she'd said!'

Ryan's arms tightened around her. 'It almost killed me
when you threw me out of your life,' he confessed. 'I
knew you were hurt because you'd lost the baby. I knew
how much it meant to you, and I knew how bitterly angry
you were because I wasn't there with you. I thought that
was why you didn't want me any more. I didn't want to
believe that you might just have grown to hate me.'

'About the baby——' she began.

'Let me finish, love.'

There was a tiny glow in her heart at the easy way the
word came to his lips. She put her head down on his
shoulder again. There was all the time in the world now.

'I hoped that if I waited, you'd get over it, and
eventually we could try again. But you didn't seem to care
if you ever saw me again, and so eventually I tried to put
the memories behind me.'

'Until the job came up,' she said.

'That's right. I really did want that job, and coming
back here was the only way I could see to get it. I thought
I'd got over you, and that it wouldn't bother me to be
around you any more.'

'You were so hateful,' she said sadly, 'and so angry.'

'From the first day I found myself struggling, and I

knew I'd been mistaken. I didn't want to fall in love with you again, Brittany, but I couldn't help myself.'

'Funny way you had of showing it,' she commented, remembering his coldness, and the sarcastic words he had flung at her.

'It was all happening over again,' he pointed out. 'From the first time I saw you, there on the campus, I wanted to take care of you—to spoil you. But your father had already done that, quite sufficiently.'

'It wasn't the money?'

He shook his head. 'Of course not. It wouldn't have mattered to me if you'd been penniless. In fact, I'd have preferred it.'

There was no denying the sincerity in his voice. Brittany sighed and snuggled a little closer to him.

'Nothing I could give you was as good as he could provide, and you kept reminding me of that.'

'You were giving me the most important thing of all,' she told him. 'Yourself. But I wasn't smart enough to see it that way, then.'

Ryan rubbed his chin against her hair. 'When we lost the baby, it seemed that everything we had was gone.'

She snapped her fingers. 'While we're talking about the baby——'

'There'll be other babies.'

'That's what I've been trying to tell you,' she said. 'The first one will arrive in about seven months. I just found out today.'

Ryan's face went chalk-white. 'Is that why you wouldn't sign the divorce papers?' he asked quietly.

'No! I want you, Ryan, but only if that's what you want as well. I've grown up that much, at least.' Then she said, in a voice that shook just a little, 'Do you want me to sign those papers?'

He smiled down at her, with that look that had always set her heart aflame. 'My dear,' he said, 'there's nothing in the world that I want more than for you to be my wife.'

'You said,' she reminded him wistfully, 'that you didn't think you were meant to be married.'

He smiled just a little. 'The idea of any other woman as my wife leaves me cold, Brittany.' He touched the tiny indentation at the base of her finger, where her wedding ring had been.

'Just let me reach it,' she said huskily, 'and I'll never take it off again.'

'Later.' It was a deeply satisfying kiss, not only a caress but a renewal of a vow made long ago and no longer to be taken lightly. It left her trembling, frightened of how close they had come to tragedy.

'We'll sell the house if you want,' she offered tentatively. The very words hurt her. Sell my pretty Castle? she thought. But there was no contest. He had called it a prison, after all, and if he felt that way, the house would only be a barrier once more.

'What? And put all these people out of work? You heartless creature!'

'We could get an apartment, maybe—just the two of us.'

'Don't you mean the three of us?' Ryan corrected softly, and she flushed pink.

'To say nothing of the fact that I can't cook,' she added demurely.

'You could learn.'

'I suppose so. And I will, if you want me to.'

'Please, Brittany!' He smiled. 'I can only take about so much humility from you.'

'I do mean it, Ryan. I have changed.'

'I know, my dear. I tried to tell myself that you were hard and cold and vicious, but I couldn't make myself believe it. And every time I looked at you I fell a little more in love.'

'This time, things are going to be as you want them.

You come first now.'

'In that case,' he said, smiling down into her eyes, 'it doesn't matter where we live, so we might as well stay here. I think I'll go see if Peters can find a log or two,' he added thoughtfully.

Brittany giggled. 'Are we having hamburgers for dinner, in front of the fireplace?'

'It would be fitting, don't you think?' He picked up the sheaf of documents from the coffee table. 'Besides, I have a bit of kindling here. Shall we burn it?'

She reached for the box of matches. 'Let's,' she said happily. 'And if that doesn't keep us warm, I have some great ideas for later!'

EPILOGUE

CHRISTMAS had come once more to the Castle. Brittany was awake early, impatient for the winter dawn. 'Come on, sleepyhead,' she teased Ryan. 'Aren't you anxious to go see your presents?'

He shook his head and pulled her down beside him. 'The only present I want is right here.' The gleam in his eyes was enough to turn her bones to water, and his kiss was lazy and languorous.

'I hate to distract you,' Brittany said.

'Then don't.'

'But the baby's going to cry at any minute.'

'Don't borrow trouble. Perhaps she'll give us a Christmas present and let us stay in bed past six o'clock for once.'

As if in answer, a sleepy little yowl came through the intercom from the nursery, followed by an angry, hungry bellow. Ryan sighed and pushed the blankets back. 'Shall we go tend to our offspring, my dear? A nanny is sounding better by the day.' Then he held up a hand as a masculine murmur soothed the child's cry, and he smiled in unholy glee. 'Your father beat us to it,' he said, and pulled Brittany back into bed.

'He must have been standing there waiting for her to wake up,' smiled Brittany. 'He was wrapped around her finger before she was born. But don't you think we should go down? It's her first Christmas, after all, and she's three months old today——'

Her protest was muffled against Ryan's mouth. Suddenly, as she relaxed against him, Christmas didn't seem to matter any more.

And much later, when they went downstairs, their baby daughter greeted them from her grandfather's knee with a bright-eyed, toothless smile, quite as if, Brittany thought, Miss Holly Masters was pleased with herself!

Take 4 novels and a surprise gift FREE

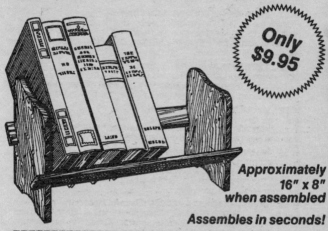

Harlequin Presents

Coming Next Month

Available in December wherever paperback books are sold, or through Harlequin Reader Service:

In the U.S.
901 Fuhrmann Blvd.
P.O. Box 1397
Buffalo, N.Y. 14240-1397

In Canada
P.O. Box 603
Fort Erie, Ontario
L2A 5X3

For the millions who can't read
Give the Gift of Literacy

One out of five adults in North America
cannot read or write well enough
to fill out a job application
or understand the directions on a bottle of medicine.

You can change all this by joining the fight
against illiteracy.

For more information write to:
Contact, Box 81826, Lincoln, Neb. 68501
In the United States, call toll free: 1-800-228-8813

The only degree you need
is a degree of caring

LIT-A-1R